ON THE EDGE

Peter Lovesey

CHIVERS PRESS
BATH

First published in Great Britain in 1989
by
Mysterious Press UK
This Large Print edition published by
Chivers Press
by arrangement with
Century Hutchinson Ltd
1991

ISBN 0 7451 3247 2

British Library Cataloguing in Publication Data available

For Jax, and more than ever by Jax

1

SMILING serenely in the September sun, Rose Bell strolled along Regent Street. Mentally she was miles away, having her husband neutered like the cat. So she ignored the woman who rushed out of Swan & Edgar's making a beeline for the kerb to hail a taxi.

The woman stopped suddenly and spun around.

'Hey, when did they let *you* out?'

Rose blinked. She registered that the woman was blonde and about her own age. A mink coat was slung casually over her shoulders. It was in beautiful condition, practically screaming out to be touched. Their eyes locked.

Rose thought, I know her, but who is she?

Penetrating eyes. Intense green. Jungle green.

Antonia Ashton.

Ack-Ack.

The service nickname struck an odd note

in peacetime 1946, but those eyes were unmistakable. In Fighter Command they'd started more scrambles than the siren.

'I can't believe it!'

Antonia came right up to her and grasped her arm.

'We've got to sit down and talk, darling. We can't just pass each other in the street.'

The first place they could find was the Black and White Milk Bar in Coventry Street. They perched on high stools under the strip lighting.

'It must be five years, at least.'

'Six.'

'Kettlesham Heath.'

'We were all completely mad.'

'We had to be.'

Antonia snapped open a gold cigarette case.

'Forgive me, darling, I spotted you straight away, but your name escapes me.'

'Rose.'

'Of course! Rose—don't tell me—Mason.'

'Not any longer.'

As Rose reached for the cigarette, Antonia leaned forward, fixed those disturbing eyes on her and lightly ran her finger down the back of her hand towards the wedding ring. 'Was it the man . . . or the money . . . or both?'

ON THE EDGE

Rose and Antonia had a good war. As WAAF plotters, they had all the excitement and independence of a difficult and dangerous job, and all the fun of being two women on an RAF base. Peacetime is a disappointment. There is rationing, shortages, and nothing to do. Rose's war-hero husband has turned brutal lout; Antonia, bored with her rich manufacturer, wants to move to America with her lover. Neither can afford a divorce. But what are plotters for if not to plot? And Antonia's ruthless scheme would give them both what they want. If Rose doesn't lose her nerve, they could get away with murder . . .

'Still smoking Abdullahs, then?'

'That's dodging the question.'

'Do you have a light?'

'Of course.' Antonia's eyes strayed to an army officer walking past the window. 'Kids?'

'No.'

'Nor me, touch wood. They're a tie, aren't they?' She produced a gold lighter and held the flame to each cigarette. 'God, this street has lost its charm. You couldn't move for GIs a year ago.'

Rose took a deep draught of smoke and immediately exhaled.

'In a hurry?'

'No, no.'

'Where were you going?'

'I heard there was a queue at Lilley & Skinner's. It was a mile long.'

'What were they like?'

'The shoes? Quite dinky. Platforms with ankle-straps. I couldn't have afforded them anyway.'

'With legs like yours you should have heels three inches high.'

'These?' Rose straightened them and looked. 'You always said potty things, Antonia, but you're a tonic.'

3

'They were the talk of 651 Squadron, and you know it.'

'Get away, if I'd known that, I'd have really larked around.'

'You?'

Antonia's eyes shone with amusement. Creases appeared at the ends of her mouth.

It was infectious. Rose started to giggle. She had to hold on to the counter to steady herself.

When two women laugh together, really laugh, nothing else matters. The rest of the world was switched off like the wireless.

'I don't know why you're laughing. You were no angel.'

'My contribution to the war effort.'

This started them off again. They took ages to subside and then Antonia made the effort to string together some intelligible words.

'Gorgeous men. I'd love to know what happened to them—the ones who came back, I mean. Rex Ballard, Johnny Dalton-Smith . . .'

'He was nice.'

'. . . and that Wing Commander who couldn't keep his hands to himself. What was his name, for heaven's sake? You remember. What a wolf! Wicked black moustache

4

and so much brilliantine it made your eyes water. Barry someone.'

'Bell.'

'Yes! Barry Bell. Run like hell, it's Barry Bell—remember?'

'I remember.'

'God knows how he ended up.'

'Married to me.'

Antonia stared.

'Darling, are you serious? You *are*.'

Rose nodded. 'After the Battle of Britain I was posted to Hornchurch. They wanted someone who could drive.'

'It's coming back to me. Didn't we give you a rather special send-off? It *was* you, wasn't it, when we all got drunk as skunks and tied your bed to the CO's staff car?'

'And didn't even tell me, rotten lot.'

'You were out to the world, sweetie. Go on, what happened at Hornchurch?'

'When I reported to the adjutant, who do you think was the first fellow I met?'

'No—really?'

'If you remember, I was about the only girl he ignored at Kettlesham Heath apart from Peggy the fat one in the NAAFI, but he said there was a reason. He said he'd been dying to ask me out and couldn't bring himself to the point.'

'Why not?'

'Because he was worried sick that I'd refuse.'

Antonia's eyes grew improbably wide. 'Barry?'

'That's what he said.'

'He worshipped you from afar? Barry? I don't mean to be personal, sweetie, but—'

'I know. I fell for it. The blue eyes, the Charles Boyer voice, the uniform, the DFC, the letter he left behind in case he was shot down. I suppose you had one, too.'

'At least you got him to the altar, which is more than the rest of us managed. How did you pull it off, or shouldn't I ask?'

'By holding out. I just said no.'

'Well done!'

'We were married during the Blitz. December, 1940. Me in parachute silk and Barry in full dress uniform complete with white gloves and sword. The next afternoon he was in a dogfight over the Channel. The funny thing is, I didn't mind. I thought it was the height of glamour bring married to a fighter pilot. Well, it was. I adored it.'

'Weren't you afraid?'

'Of what? A telephone call? Of course, but that's something the plucky little woman had to accept in wartime, didn't she?'

Antonia put her hand to her mouth.

'He wasn't . . . ?'

'Killed in action? No. Not Barry. He came through without a scratch.'

'And you're still happily married?'

'Still married.'

Antonia inhaled on her cigarette and gave Rose a long speculative look.

'He was demobbed last February.'

'And?'

'He's in the civil service. The Stationery Office. A distribution officer. Sounds impressive, but he's only a clerk in reality.'

'I can't picture Barry as a civil servant.'

'It is quite a transformation. You should see him go off each day with his bowler hat and briefcase.'

'He was such an outgoing chap.'

'You mean no girl was safe with him. He hasn't altered in that respect.'

'It hasn't worked out?'

'It's a mess.'

'I'm sorry, darling. Will you . . . ?'

'Divorce him? I couldn't face a divorce at the moment. It would break Daddy's heart.'

'But it's *your* life.'

'Daddy married us in his own church, heard the vows, gave us the blessing.'

Antonia pointed a finger. 'Your pa was a vicar. I remember now!'

Rose had started talking about herself to show she was friendly and now all this had gushed out. It was embarrassing. She needed to broaden the conversation. 'I sometimes wish the war had never ended, don't you?'

'We're no better off, if that's what you mean.'

Rose ran her eyes over the mink. 'Aren't we?'

Antonia dismissed that with a shrug. 'I mean the bloody shortages. What happened to domestic servants? You can't get one for love nor money.'

Rose smiled. 'I haven't tried.'

'Take rationing, then. I couldn't run my car to the end of the street on the petrol they allow you.' Antonia said all this with a straight face. She looked at the cigarette in her hand. 'And the things you have to do for a smoke.'

'You've got a *car?*'

She nodded.

'Who on earth did you marry—a duke?'

Antonia flicked off some ash. 'You wouldn't know him. Hector wasn't one of our crowd. He wasn't in the services.

8

Reserved occupation. Do you know that air-raid shelter in Chelsea near the Five Bells? We both ducked in there when a V-1 was overhead. It exploded while we were still halfway down the steps and I grabbed him.' She grinned. 'I felt better pressed up to his wallet.'

Rose giggled. She'd always found Antonia fun and admired her nerve. She'd never listened to the jealous WAAFs who lost their men to her.

'Did it take long?'

'April. We had to wait for his wife to die.'

'Was she an invalid?'

'Maudie? No. She drowned.'

Rose caught her breath. The *non sequitur*, tossed out so casually, perplexed her. She couldn't think what to say next. It would have been in bad taste to press for more information, and Antonia didn't volunteer any.

Antonia blew out a thin shaft of smoke and coolly took up the conversation.

'So you and I end up like this.'

'Like what?'

'Two bored housewives wishing we were back in the filter room at Kettlesham Heath.'

'I don't know about that. It was no picnic. Night duty. Those beastly earphones. Bend-ing over the map to get our plots down. I don't know which was worse, the earache or the backache.'

'Think of the compensations—the boys in the gallery.'

'Don't! I daydream far too much.'

'Listen, Rose, I've got to go in a tick. Why don't we do this again?'

'Oh, I don't know if I can.'

'But you'd like to?'

'Well, yes.'

'So we will.'

Antonia took a taxi to Knightsbridge and let herself into a first-floor flat in Basil Street, behind Harrods. A man's voice called from the end of a red-carpeted passage.

'Tea?'

'Just had some.'

'Who with?'

'Someone I happened to meet in Piccadilly.'

'Someone interesting?'

'A plotter.'

He appeared at the door, Italian in looks, but taller than most Italians.

'A what?'

'One of the WAAFs I knew in the war.

We used to push metal arrows around an enormous map.'

'A *plotter*.'

Antonia tossed the mink over a satin-cushioned chair.

'Her name is Rose.'

'Nice-looking?'

'Simmer down, man. As a matter of fact she is quite pretty in a pure-bred English way. Soft brown hair in natural curls. Wonderful skin. Bright eyes with long lashes. She'd have made a very presentable deb in her day. I can see her looking out at me from the pages of the *Tatler*. Have I put you off yet?'

'Totally and utterly.'

'Good.'

'Will you see her again?'

'Next week.'

He smiled.

'What's funny?'

'Two plotters with nothing left to plot.'

'Not necessarily. What's the time now?'

'Nearly half past four. Thinking about your husband?'

'Vic darling, don't make me laugh.'

She started unbuttoning her blouse.

2

Rose stood by the kitchen table in her apron waiting for her husband to get up from his armchair. The *Evening Standard* was full of murder again and Barry was lapping up every word. He'd followed each day of the trial of Neville Heath, the man just sentenced to death for suffocating a woman in a London hotel after beating her with a riding switch. It now came out that Heath had committed a second sadistic killing. Most of Britain— the newspapers anyway—had been engrossed by the case, as if the war hadn't given them enough death and violence. Rose found it sickening, but she was in the minority. And Barry claimed an interest because Heath was an ex-pilot in the South African Air Force who had spent some months with the RAF, attached to 180 Squadron. There was, admittedly, a suggestion of reflected glory about the way he spoke of him.

'By God, he's a handsome devil.'

'Your supper's getting cold.'

'You've got to admit he's handsome. Look.' He held the paper up. Heath was pictured seated between two detectives in the back of a car.

Not my idea of handsome, Rose thought, but a sight better-looking than you, I'll grant you, with your boozer's nose and flabby cheeks and overgrown moustache. 'It'll be ruined.'

'They tried to save him from the hangman by saying he was mad. Believe me, this chappie is as sane as you and me. Any man who can pilot a Mitchell bomber must be all right in the head.'

'Barry, are you coming to the table or not?'

'I never thought the day would come when a bloody murderer wore the RAF tie at his trial. You give a chap his wings and he behaves like that. Lunatic.'

'You just contradicted yourself.'

'What I'm saying is that he wasn't fit to hold the King's Commission.'

'He wasn't the only one.'

'Cow.'

'I didn't mean you. I'll say that for you— you were a bloody good officer once.'

He hadn't listened. He was back with his newspaper. She could have added that he was the world's worst civil servant, but she didn't. He knew it.

Why antagonize him? He only passed on his frustration by humiliating her.

When Vic had a short lunch break he would meet Antonia in the Trevor Arms in Knightsbridge, ten minutes or so from Imperial College, where he lectured. He always whistled at the prices but it was the only pub in the district with carpets and soft lighting and barmaids who called you 'sir', and Antonia preferred it to anywhere else.

Today he offered her a gin and It instead of the usual shandy.

She raised her eyebrows. 'What's all this for, naughty boy? No point in getting me sloshed if you're going straight back to your boring students.'

'Is it no, then?'

'That's a little word I never use.'

She was getting some looks as usual. She was always being told she had a carrying voice. She leaned back in her chair and winked at a chinless lieutenant who was staring over his shoulder. The Trevor was the unofficial officers' mess for the Life Guards, who had their barracks next door.

Vic returned with the drinks. 'Actually

I've got good news. Well, good news for me in a way.'

'Let's hear it, then.'

'I've been offered a two-year temporary lectureship at Princeton.'

Antonia put down her glass. 'Princetown? Someone's led you up the garden path, darling. That's not a university. It's a prison in the middle of Dartmoor.'

'Princeton, New Jersey.'

She felt a prickling sensation in her scalp. 'America?'

He nodded.

'For two years?'

'It's not until next summer.'

She looked into his brown eyes. Mentally he was already over there in New Jersey. She was livid. She couldn't survive a day without him. He was *it*. She'd never known a man who excited her more. 'You bastard! You didn't tell me you applied for this.'

'I didn't think I stood an earthly. Look, Antonia, it's not the end of the world.'

How little he knew! 'Judas! Two-faced, scurvy, bloodsucking louse. I'm coming with you.'

He was back in London like a rocket. 'You can't do that. You know you can't.'

'Who says?'

15

'You're married.'

'I'll leave him.'

Those eyes of his opened so wide she could see white all round them. 'It's an Ivy League university. I couldn't turn up there with a married woman in tow.'

As promised, Antonia was by the band-stand at half past two, conspicuous in a lilac-coloured coat with bishop sleeves and a matching Breton sailor hat tilted back rak-ishly. She was getting some long looks from the nannies walking their prams.

'Let's go that way, towards the Mall.'

'It's all the same to me.'

Green Park no longer looked like a war zone. The bulldozers had flattened the barbed wire fences and the searchlight sta-tion and filled in the artificial lake in time for the Victory celebrations. Squads of Ital-ian POWs had laid fresh turf. Today London-ers in scores were out enjoying the autumn sun.

Rose gossiped happily about old times, and Antonia chipped in with bits of news she had picked up since. They covered just about everyone of the Kettlesham Heath crowd. Almost an hour passed before Antonia switched back to the present.

16

'Where do you and Barry live, then?'

Rose considered what answer she would give. She chose to keep it vague. 'Out Pimlico way.'

'A house? One of those sweet little terraced boxes covered in stucco?' Antonia should have been in intelligence in the war.

'It was all we could get and now we've got to stay until the war damage is put right.'

'So you were bombed.'

'The house across the street. A doodlebug. No one was hurt, thank God, but we lost our front door and all the windows and there are cracks you can see daylight through.'

'Bloody doodlebugs.'

'It could have been much worse. You have to look on the bright side. We can see right across the river now.' And I, Rose instantly thought, am incapable of keeping any secrets at all. I didn't want to tell her all this. She tried clumsily to cover up. 'But no one can ever find us because we haven't got a number on the new door.'

'No number?'

'No number.' Rose raised a smile. 'We don't do much entertaining.'

'You might get a visit from me one of these days.'

'Don't! I'd die of shame if you turned up.'

17

'Did you tell Barry you met me?'

'No. I didn't mention it.'

'Don't you two have much to say to each other?'

'The only thing he wants to talk about is that revolting murder in the papers.'

'Neville Heath. How dull.'

'Dull? I call it horrible.'

'He's a psychopath, of course.'

'Heath?'

'Well, I wasn't referring to Barry, darling.'

There was a moment before Rose spoke again.

'What's a psychopath?'

Antonia responded as if to a child. 'He has a diseased mind, my dear.'

'Obviously.'

'So what can be more dull than that? He was incapable of committing an intelligent murder. Darling, are those rain clouds, would you say?'

They took the straightest route back to Piccadilly, where Antonia insisted on tea in the Palm Court at the Ritz. In the pink and gold setting her outfit looked so exquisite that she must have known all the time she would come here. Rose, seated in front of a gilded water nymph on a rock, felt like a refugee in her green tweed coat and woollen headscarf. People at other tables glanced at her and looked away.

'I shouldn't have come in.'

'My dear, nobody's taking any notice.'

'I do have better things at home.'

'Imagine how *I* felt in the Black and White Milk Bar.'

'If only I'd known we were coming here.'

'Relax. We deserve this.'

'I'm not sure why.'

'For putting up with our ghastly husbands.'

Rose forgot what she was wearing for a moment.

'Is yours a problem too?'

'Hector?' Antonia tensed suddenly and lowered her voice. 'Don't look now, but I think a fellow over there is giving one of us the eye.'

'Oh, no. Where?'

'To your left against the window, sitting alone. Grey pinstripe. Clark Gable moustache.'

Rose stole a glance.

'For pity's sake, Antonia! He's sixty if he's a day.'

'I swear to God that's an American tie. Where would he get a tie like that in England? It *is* Clark Gable. And he's looking at you.'

'Dressed like this?'

'Americans go wild over tweeds. This is your chance, darling. Show him some stocking and let's see if he comes over.'

Any uncertainty in Rose's mind was removed. This was a well-tried game of Antonia's, picking out the most unlikely men and casting them as heart-throbs for her friends. Amusing to everyone but the victim. She was always catching people.

'Cool down, Ack-Ack, this isn't the sergeants' mess.'

'He's panting for you.'

'Panting! He's hardly breathing. He's practically asleep. His eyes are closing. Look, he's closed his eyes.'

'*Imagining* things.'

Antonia's face was so suggestive, and the whole thing so ridiculous that Rose was forced to smile and it started Antonia off. She made sounds like a traction engine picking up steam. Rose snatched a hankie to her mouth.

'He is definitely asleep.'

'He's just pretending.'

'He's sliding down his chair. Any minute now he's going to slip under the table.'

'Don't let that fool you. He's trying to see up your skirt.'

Rose reddened and tugged the hem over her knees.

'Spoilsport.'

Before they left, a waiter handed a small white cake-box to Antonia. She thanked him and put a coin in his hand. Then she turned to Rose.

'Isn't it a bore trying to think of things to feed the cat with? I find cream quite impossible to get in the shops.'

The umbrellas were up when they came out. There wasn't a taxi in sight, so they stood under the arcade and waited for the shower to stop. Rose didn't mind. She didn't want the afternoon to end. It was like old times, only better. Antonia wasn't performing for an entire hutful of WAAFs. The entertainment was for private delectation. She couldn't tell what to believe, and she was captivated.

Antonia hadn't finished, either.

'You and I will definitely have to do something about our husbands.'

'Do what?'

'Get shot of them.'

The only way to cope with Antonia in this mood was to keep a straight face and treat

everything she said with total seriousness—
until you collapsed laughing.

'How do you mean—get shot of them?'

Antonia flicked her hand as if she were
shaking off the rain.

Rose aped the action. 'Just like that?'

'More or less.'

'Difficult, I should think.'

'Not at all.'

'I told you I'm not getting a divorce.'

'I wasn't talking about divorce.'

'All right, cleversticks, what other way is
there to get shot of a husband?'

'I can think of at least a dozen.'

'Name one, then.'

'A fatal accident.'

'Small chance of that!'

'Chance needn't come into it, darling.
Quick, that taxi's pulling up.'

The Ritz commissionaire beckoned to
them with his white glove. He seemed to
know Antonia. He waved away some other
people and held a huge brown umbrella over
them as they climbed in.

At home she tuned in to the Light Pro-
gramme, got *Merry-Go-Round* and started the
ironing. Barry's shirts had to be ready for
another week. She couldn't imagine Antonia

at the ironing board these days, though she'd seen her often enough in the billet at Kettlesham Heath pressing her uniform for kit inspections and her civvies for dates with the officers. Things had moved on since then.

Antonia has, at any rate, Rose reflected. As for me, I've slipped. Those really were better times. We bleated about the food and the uniforms, but we had some point to our lives. Women had a part to play in fighting the war. We were needed. And they paid us.

I was happy. Even the first years of marriage to Barry weren't too impossible. I still had some self-respect and so did he. And the joke of it is that we all looked forward to something called Victory Day.

Victory!

It was Friday and Barry wouldn't be in before ten. He always picked up a woman after work on Fridays. She spat on the flat-iron to see if it was hot enough. A far cry from afternoon tea at the Ritz. She picked a shirt from the heap and spread it out, dipped her fingers in a basin of water and flicked her hand over the shirt.

'Just like that.'

She watched the droplets darken and spread.

3

HECTOR was holding forth about the Britain Can Make It Exhibition as a shop window for his products, which Antonia thought was rich considering he was a Czech. She smiled at a couple at another table and said something about the weather and Hector didn't even pause for breath. She reached across the table and pulled his plate away.

It got a reaction. 'Hey, what are you doing?'

'Haven't you finished? I have.'

'That's my dinner you took away.'

'It'll walk away by itself if you carry on much longer.'

'What do you mean?'

'Never mind.' She handed back the plate.

'I forget what I said now.'

'Good. Will you give me a divorce?'

'What?'

'I want a divorce, Hec. I want to marry Vic and go to America. He's been offered a job at Princeton University.'

Hector chuckled and brought the dimples to his cheeks, which always infuriated Antonia because it made her feel like a cradle-snatcher. In reality he was twelve years her senior, yet such a shrimp that people thought of him as not much over twenty. His springy red hair was the sort that looked no different after it was combed. 'Vic is leaving? Your fancy man is leaving?'

'I'm going with him. I'm getting a divorce from you and going with him.'

'Not possible.'

A harsher note came through in her voice. 'You're going to say it's against your religion, aren't you? Listen. You don't go to Mass. You don't make confessions. You're not exactly one of the flock, sweetie.'

'Christmas I go to Mass.'

'Face it, Hector, you've lapsed.'

'Do I treat you bad?'

'We're bored with each other. Admit it. We made a mistake.'

'This is possible. Divorce is not. We will stay married till death. Understand?'

She took a gulp of wine and leaned forward in her chair. 'Have you thought of this, Hec? If you gave me grounds, I could divorce you. It's not against *my* religion.'

'Grounds? What are you talking about? I

don't understand what you need grounds for if you want to leave the country.'

'Grounds—a reason, sweetie, not a piece of land. Misconduct, as they put it in the papers. You'd simply pay some woman to spend the night in a hotel with you.'

He laughed again. 'You make it sound like money for jam. How much do such women charge? Five pounds? Ten? You think I'm a complete chump? It isn't just a divorce you're planning. You want costs. And maintenance. For ever and ever. You want to carry on eating in restaurants and buying expensive clothes. I may not be a great husband, Antonia, but I'm a pretty good businessman, and that's bad business, terrible business. No deal. No divorce. For-get it.'

She said, 'Bastard. I'll just leave you.' But the words didn't carry conviction.

Already he was talking about the bloody exhibition again. The people on an adjacent stand had told him that Prestcold were plan-ning to have domestic refrigerators back on the market within a year—far more disturb-ing to Hector than the prospect of his wife abandoning him.

All around them in the glitter and red

plush of Reggiori's, couples were gazing dewy-eyed at each other over the wine.

'. . . I could speed up production easy, but I depend on suppliers, you see. I give you this example. Take aluminium alloy.'

'Hector.'

'Essential in manufacture.'

'Hector I've got a question for you. A technical question.

'You have?'

'How many volts of electricity do they use in the underground?'

'Over six hundred. Nominally six hundred and thirty DC. Why do you ask this?'

'Enough to kill someone?'

'Easy.' He grinned. 'But I never use the tube, so you'd better think of some other thing.'

Antonia smiled back serenely. 'Ah, but I might be thinking of suicide, mightn't I, little man?'

'You?' This amused him greatly. 'You've got to know which rails to jump on.'

'The live rail.'

He handed his plate to a passing waiter and removed the cruet from the centre of the table, welcoming the rare chance to impress his wife with some electrical knowhow. 'Pass me those knives.' He arranged four knives

27

in parallel between them. 'Now, two long knives—this and this—represent running rails, understand?'

'The wheels of the train move along them.'

'Good. Small knives are conductor rails.'

'*Two* live rails?'

'Positive and negative. Positive goes between the running rails, negative outside them. In a station'—he moved his place mat alongside the knives— 'the negative conductor rail is right over there, along the opposite wall. Now, you want to electrocute yourself. For best results, you should be in contact with both conductor rails at the same time.'

Antonia frowned. 'I'd need to be an athlete or a contortionist.'

'Difficult, yes.'

'What would happen if you just hit the nearest conductor rail?'

'In theory you could still earth six hundred and thirty volts.'

'And in practice?'

Hector smiled and pressed the tablecloth with both hands to make a furrow between the knives. 'Here, below the rails in each station they have a pit. The suicide pit. Chances are that you will fall between the rails.'

'Without getting a shock? This isn't very helpful, Hec. People *do* get killed sometimes, so how does it happen?'

'Simple. They jump in front of the train, so it's not electrocution that kills them.'

She pulled a face. 'Messy.'

He laughed. 'You want to look pretty in your coffin? You'd better take phenobarbitone.'

Rose had been in bed an hour when the key turned in the front door. Barry took each stair as if it were put there to trap him, then loosed a huge belch as he passed the bedroom door on his way to the bathroom. This, she reflected, is the Battle of Britain hero, the dashing fighter pilot I promised to love and cherish.

So how will I deal with him? I'll pretend I'm asleep. I don't want a scene. Probably I won't even mention it tomorrow. The plain truth is that I'm resigned to this every Friday night. I'm resigned to being ignored when he's home every other night of the week, so why should I object when he stays out and comes home drunk?

I'm trapped in this nightmare. I haven't just slipped in my standard of living since the war. I've slipped mentally. I've practically given up.

He thrust open the door and switched on the light.

Rose closed her eyes.

She heard him lurch to the bed, then felt his hand on her shoulder. He turned her over. She opened her eyes. He stood swaying there in his braces, no collar attached to his shirt.

'Bloody trains.'

'Where are your waistcoat and jacket?'

'Bathroom.'

She got out of bed to retrieve them. If she could possibly help it, there wouldn't be a scene. Fixing her mind on the things she regarded as the duties of a wife helped to control her anger. It was a woman's job to keep her husband decently kitted for work. He owned this blue pinstripe and his demob suit and one pre-war flannel monstrosity that he refused to part with.

The waistcoat and jacket lay in a heap beside the lavatory. Mechanically she picked several long fair hairs off the sleeves and dropped them into the bowl. She shook the jacket and something rattled in a side pocket. She took out a hotel key and glanced at the disc, replaced it and took the clothes to a hanger in the wardrobe.

He was face down on the bed, still in his day things.

'Are you proposing to sleep in your trousers?'

He made a show of clawing the braces off his shoulders.

'Roll over.'

She unbuttoned him at the front and peeled off the trousers.

He tugged the bedding aside and crawled underneath.

'Had a few after work.'

She emptied his pocket and placed the loose change in the ashtray on the chest of drawers. She smoothed the trousers and lined up the creases.

'You don't have to explain.'

'What time is it?'

'Some time after midnight.'

'Quite a bit later than usual.'

'Yes.'

She clamped the trousers in the wooden press beside the tallboy. She knew why he was late. Not because he had had a few whiskys after work. The drinking was incidental to his pursuit of women. She knew all about his infidelities. She was used to being looked at by friends in a certain way and told that her husband had been sighted again in the bar of the Strand Palace Hotel. They didn't have to say any more. The entire scene was in the look.

What had delayed him then? One thing was certain: it wasn't an excess of passion. He couldn't contain himself for more than a minute even when sober. He was late because he'd gone to a different hotel, in Hammersmith. Presumably he'd failed to find a pick-up in the West End. So he'd started again. More whiskys. More than he could handle.

He was making an effort to sound rational.

'Did you get worried about me?'

'Worried?'

'I mean, did you think I'd had an accident?'

'An accident?' Her conversation with Antonia outside the Ritz flitted into her mind and out of it. 'No.'

'Callous bitch.'

'Barry, you're in no state—'

'I could have been dead for all you care. You don't bloody care, do you?'

He was working himself up. *She* was angry, too, and entitled to be. What was picking his clothes off the floor if it wasn't caring? Rescuing his clothes that reeked of some woman and dutifully hanging them up for him. Yet she didn't want an argument. She took her dressing-gown off the hook.

'I'm going to sleep in the spare room.'

She reached to pick up her pillow and with surprising speed he grabbed her wrist and jerked her off balance. She fell across the bed.

'You're staying here and that's an order.'

'Barry, let go of my arm.'

He started wrestling with her. She was pushed face down into the eiderdown. She was shocked by the force of the attack. He had never been violent before. She twisted her head for breath and she felt her nightdress tearing at the armpit. He clapped his hand on the back of her neck.

'Don't you dare move, woman.'

'Barry, you're hurting.'

'You don't know what it is to be hurt.'

His voice had a cruel edge she had never heard from him. A horrid possibility crept into her mind. His imagination had been stoked up by the newspapers reporting those vile murders by Heath.

'Please, Barry.'

'Getting above yourself, aren't you? Bloody vicar's daughter. Need bringing down a peg or two.'

He slid his hand upwards, took a grip on her hair and twisted her head with such force that her shoulders and torso followed the movement. She was turned face up like a playing card. His leg straddled her thighs and trapped her. Whisky fumes gusted into her face.

She was rigid with fear, certain he meant to bite her. She could see the teeth bared.

'Barry, no!'

'Shut up.'

His face moved closer, rasping her cheek with his moustache. He spoke in her ear.

'You're a sanctimonious bitch. Admit it. Out with it, loud and clear.'

'Please—'

'Say it.'

'I'm a sanctimonious bitch.'

'Louder. Tell the neighbours what you are. Tell the whole bloody street.'

She shouted the words.

'Better. And you were worried sick when I was late.'

'I was worried sick.'

'Why?'

'Why what?'

'Come on. Why were you worried sick?'

He was speaking between clenched teeth. He expected an answer fast. And this time he expected her to supply it.

Her face twitched. She was too terrified to think.

'Come on!'

'I thought . . .'

'Yes?'

'I thought you must have had an accident.'

'What sort of accident?'

'What sort?'

'I want to know if you're speaking the truth. You say you thought I had an accident.'

She couldn't fathom what satisfaction this gave him and she dreaded where it was leading. She just hoped to God she could keep the right answers coming. If it spared her from physical pain she was willing to supply whatever he wanted to hear.

She blurted out the first thing she could think of. 'Er—an accident on some stairs. You fell down some stairs and broke your leg.'

'Where?'

'I don't know—the office.'

'They'd have let you know. Someone

would have let you know by seven, easily. Better think again.'

'You fell off a bus. You hit your head on the road and got concussion. Nobody knew who you were.'

'So what did my poor distracted wife do about it?'

'Phoned the police. And all the hospitals.'

'How touching. And all this is true, isn't it, Rose, darling, because you were brought up to believe that lying is a sin before God?' He pressed his forefinger under her chin and pushed upwards. 'Have I caught you out?'

'I'm confused. I don't know what you want me to say.'

'Say you were lying through your teeth.'

'All right, I was.'

'And I caught you at it.'

'You caught me at it.'

This appeared to satisfy him, because he gave a grunt and withdrew the leg that was pinning her down. He rolled right away from her and sat up.

'I'm going for a piss. Don't move a muscle.'

Rose's nerves gave way to the stress. She shivered uncontrollably. Too fearful to run out, she dreaded his return. She listened to him pass water, then flush the cistern. It was all she could do to stop from whimpering when he came back. Yet she still had sufficient detachment to despise herself. That made it harder to endure, knowing what a spineless creature she had become.

He turned out the light as he came in. Then he dropped on to the bed like a felled tree, on his own side, close to Rose, without touching. She prayed that he might sleep now, but he still wanted to taunt her.

'What a flaming liar! I said what a flaming liar! Lord bloody Haw-Haw isn't in it. Let's face it, you wouldn't lose any sleep if I ended up in hospital. You were nicely tucked up in bed when I finally got in, weren't you? Weren't you?'

'Is that what upset you? I didn't realize.'

She felt slightly easier in her mind for finding a reason for his behaviour. She hadn't pictured it from his point of view. He wasn't home by midnight so she had gone to bed. Evidently he regarded this as a betrayal. It was the silliest nonsense considering how he had spent the evening, but that was the way his mind worked. He felt rejected. God, what she was reduced to!

'Shall I make you some coffee?'

'Coffee be buggered.'

'Just as you wish.'

'I'm accident-proof, if you want to know. I got through the war without a prang, didn't I? Over seven hundred flying hours. After that I'm not going to fall down the moving staircase at Victoria, am I? Or walk into a lamp post.' He made a smug chuckling sound. 'The only accident I ever had was with a certain WAAF sergeant at Hornchurch.'

She tensed again. 'What do you mean?'

He could hardly speak for laughing now. The words came out in a wheeze.

'You know what I mean. An accident. One that got away. A bun in the oven.'

'You got her pregnant?'

'That was the upshot, so to speak.'

Rose's hands crept up to her neck.

'She had a child?'

'A bouncing baby boy.'

'At Hornchurch? After we were married.' She sat up in bed in the dark. 'You had a child after we were married? You're lying.'

'Who are you calling a liar? There's only one liar in this house, and it isn't me.'

4

ANTONIA was emphatic. 'Darling, he made the whole thing up.'

'Don't you believe it?'

'It's absolute rubbish.'

'Listen, he told me the woman's name—Stella Paxton. She was in the MT section at Hornchurch, driving the officers about.'

'Does that prove anything?'

'But Barry's quite open about his affairs. Why would he lie about this?'

'Men have fragile egos, my flower. He came in late expecting a scene and you put him to bed like your tame teddy bear. He was insulted.'

'You think he wanted a scene?'

'A fight, more like.'

'That's rich. Here am I wondering where I went wrong and you tell me I didn't pick a fight. We've never had fights.'

'And look at the result.'

In spite of her distress, Rose smiled. She'd phoned because she needed to speak

39

to someone. It wasn't the sort of problem you could take to your mother and father. She knew she could rely on Antonia for a heart-to-heart and some cogent advice.

'Would you have given him a telling-off?'

'A telling-off! A punch in the kisser. He wanted a reaction.'

'He's got one now—I'm devastated.'

'Of course you are, poor lamb. You've taken it all to heart.'

'He hurt me. Physically held me down and hurt me. I was terrified and he knew it.'

'It's just a game to them. They don't know their own strength.'

'Not Barry. He isn't like that. I thought he was going to strike me.'

'But he didn't?'

'Well no.'

'All right, he scared you a bit. Didn't the boys at school ever chase you with a spider or something? It's horrid, but it's not without excitement.'

'You don't understand. There was nothing playful about this. It was vile, as if . . . . Oh, I don't know. Perhaps it's my imagination. That beastly murder in the newspapers is giving me ideas.'

'Heath?'

'I told you. Barry's fascinated by it.'

40

'Sounds as if *he* was the one who got ideas.'

'Antonia, I don't believe he made it up about Stella Paxton and the baby.'

'If that's what worries you, you'd better find out for sure.'

'Yes, but how?'

'Go through his things for heaven's sake.'

'I can't do that.'

'Don't be naïve, flower. If he has another woman and child and he's thinking of ditching you . . .'

'Oh, I didn't say that.'

'. . . don't you think you have a right to know? Does he keep letters, photographs, anything like that?'

'He keeps the bills in the writing desk. I've no idea what else is in there.,

'Better get busy then. Is it locked?'

'The lock isn't very good.'

'Well, then. Put down the phone and do it now. Barry isn't there, is he?'

'Of course not, but I've always respected his privacy.'

'Did he respect you when he got Stella Paxton pregnant?'

Rose closed her eyes tightly. 'Now you're telling me it's true. I don't know what to believe. Antonia, what do you really think?'

41

'Never mind me, sweetie. It's obvious you've got to find out for yourself.'

She still hesitated when it came to forcing open the desk. Her throat went dry and her hand on the kitchen knife trembled.

She hesitated because the act of breaking into Barry's desk was underhanded. She had been deceived; now she was trading deceit for deceit.

'Did he respect you . . . ?'

She tightened her grip, slid the knife in and pressed on it, supporting the flap with her left hand as it came open. Everything was stacked in front of her in the slots and shelves—bills, chequebooks, bank statements, payslips, his demob papers, photos, marriage certificate and bundles of business letters. There were fountain pens, bottles of ink, a glass paperweight and the case containing his DFC.

Ashamed of herself, she snapped the desk shut again.

She returned to the kitchen, put the knife back in the drawer and took out the small bottle of brandy that she kept in the larder. It was supposed to be for Christmas puddings, but she usually forgot to use it. It had come in useful when her mother stayed with her during the bombing. She poured some into a medicine glass.

The phone rang. She knew it would be Antonia again.

'What did you find, darling?'

'Nothing at all.'

'Really? You did get into the desk, I hope?'

'Yes.'

'I'm surprised, then. Did you find his address book?'

'Address book? No.'

'Diaries, letters?'

'Nothing of a personal nature.'

'He keeps them somewhere else, then. Can you think of any other place?'

'Not at the moment. Look, I'm going to give it some thought before I do anything else.'

'We'll work something out between us.'

'Thanks awfully, Antonia, but I ought to think this out carefully before I do anything at all.'

'Don't be so daft, darling. What are friends for? We'll sort it out tomorrow.'

'Tomorrow?'

'Elevenses in the Corner House.'

'Would you mind terribly if we didn't? I'm still rather shaky. I don't feel up to going out.'

'You poor wee thing—of course. How about Thursday?'

'I'd rather leave it for the present if you don't mind. Perhaps in a week or two.'

She wasn't too proud of herself for putting Antonia off so soon after turning to her for support, but she didn't want to be hustled into doing things against her conscience. It hadn't been right to force open the writing desk. She would find out the truth by some less underhanded means. The most obvious way was to ask Barry straight out, but she couldn't face that. It would be laying herself open to more hurt. She wanted to know, but not in the heat of argument.

5

ANTONIA didn't hang up the phone directly. She rang for a taxi. There was just time to change into a blue double-breasted suit and pink frilly blouse and to touch up her lips before the cab pulled up at the door.

'The tobacconist's in Sloane Square.'

There, she winked at the solemn old Scot who supplied her with ciggies.

'Have they come in yet?' She could always rely on him for a packet of some brand or other, even with the shortages. Today it was ten Escudos, passed over the counter in a brown paper bag.

'They're one and threepence, I'm afraid.'

'That's all right. How are your Hearts, Mr MacDade?'

'Disappointing, madam. They lost four nil at home last week.'

'Just what they needed, darling. Football players are like carpets—they need the occasional beating. They'll score a hatful on Saturday.'

'Is that a fact?'

She got back into the taxi.

'Pimlico, please.'

'What address, lady?'

'Perhaps you can tell me. A street where a flying bomb fell.'

'I'm a cabbie, love, not the ARP.'

'It can't be so difficult to find. The house I want is in a terrace opposite the bomb site. And it faces the river.'

They drove to Pimlico and looked for someone to ask. Every street was a porticoed terrace. A woman with a pram knew of two bomb sites. An entire terrace had been flattened in Sutherland Street and twenty people had been killed, but that was in the Blitz. Her second suggestion turned out to have been the result of high-explosive bombs in 1943. A milkman suggested Oldfield Gardens. He thought it was a doodlebug that had flattened the end house there.

Oldfield Gardens had a down-at-heel look. Some of the shabbiness was the result of war damage; much more could be put down to neglect. The houses had once looked smart with their casement windows, solid front doors and iron railings around the basement steps. Cheap replacement doors had spoilt the effect and the once-white fronts were chipped and stained.

She asked the driver to wait by the corner shop at the end of the street farthest from the bomb site. The smell of cats crept into her nostrils.

A wolf-whistle greeted her as she approached the bomb site. Some workmen were fixing posts into what had once been a front garden. She gave them a wave and crossed the road.

The last house was unusual for not having an array of doorbells. The doorstep was polished to inspection standard. She pressed the bell.

She flung out her hands and embraced Rose the moment she opened the door.

'My poor flower—I couldn't abandon

you at a time like this. I've brought you some ciggies.'

Rose muttered some words of thanks as Antonia broke off the embrace and headed for the scullery.

'What a sweet house, and so tastefully furnished. Is it all yours? I love it.'

'I've got rather a headache.'

'I'll make you some tea. No, I insist. You sit down and I'll do everything. Have you got any aspirin? I can bring it upstairs if you'd like to lie down.'

She filled the kettle and lit the gas and then wandered out to look at the other rooms, calling out her observations as she went.

'Oh, a piano. Do you play, darling? I can't believe Barry likes Sigmund Romberg. He said a beautiful thing—Romberg, not Barry—"A love song is just a caress set to music." Isn't that romantic? And this must be the writing desk you mentioned.'

'Please don't touch the writing desk.'

'I wouldn't dream of it.'

'I don't mean to be rude.'

'Be as rude as you like, my pet. That's what I keep telling you—you're too polite for your own good.'

The phone rang in the front room where Antonia was.

'Leave it to me, darling.' She picked up the receiver and put it to her ear.

A man's voice, cautious and well-spoken.

'Good morning, is that Wing Commander Bell?'

'I'm afraid not. Can I help?'

'Roberts here. Manager of the Westminster Bank.'

'Yes?'

'I really wished to speak to him personally on a confidential matter. Am I speaking to Mrs Bell, by any chance?'

Antonia decided that a white lie was not only excusable, but opportune.

'Well, yes.'

'I wonder . . . is your husband away from home?'

'Away? No. He's at work.'

'Only I've sent a number of letters over the last month asking him to come and see me, and received no reply.'

'I'm sure there's a reason.'

'Undoubtedly.'

'I'll ask him to get in touch.'

'Would you? These things are better discussed man to man, so to speak. I'm sure we'll reach an amicable arrangement.'

'I hope so.'

'Thank you. Goodbye, Mrs Bell.'

She heard the click and the purring note before she replaced the receiver, thinking about the amicable arrangement that Barry was expected to reach with his bank manager. She returned to the kitchen as the kettle was boiling.

'That was Mr Roberts, the manager of the Westminster Bank.'

'Really? What did he want?'

'A word with Barry. I told him he wasn't here.'

'Stupid man. What does he expect if he rings up in the middle of the morning?'

'He's written several letters.'

'To Barry? Yes, he has. One arrived this morning.'

'He's been asking Barry to come and see him. Barry hasn't replied.'

'I can't understand that. He's awfully efficient. I wonder what this is about.'

Antonia handed her a cup of tea. 'It's staring you in the face, sweetie. He's overdrawn at the bank.'

'That's impossible. We live quite frugally. I haven't had a new dress since the war and he's still wearing the same suit. We don't even use our clothing coupons.'

'What about his nights out?'

'Oh, he doesn't believe in spending much

on his women. Never more than a couple of drinks and the price of a cheap hotel room for an hour. It's a matter of pride with Barry.'

'In that case, I apologize.'

'What for?'

'For misleading you. Obviously I was wrong.'

'About what?'

'For pity's sake, darling—the child. There *is* a child. Barry's in the red because he's keeping up two households. You can't do that on the money a civil service clerk takes home.'

Rose put down her cup. The colour drained from her face. It was a long time before she spoke and then her voice came as a whisper.

'It's not true.'

Antonia took an unopened letter from behind the clock on the mantelpiece, glanced at the typed address and then propped it against Rose's teacup. Rose shook her head.

'I couldn't. He'd know.'

Antonia took out her lighter and put the flame to the gas ring. Steam gushed from the kettle again. She picked up the letter and held the back of it to the spout.

'He won't find out.'

When it was quite moist, she placed the

letter in Rose's hand, at the same time squeezing her arm.

Rose started peeling back the flap.

'From the bottom, darling. You don't want to tear it.'

She took out the letter, read it and threw it down.

'He's overdrawn six hundred and ninety pounds, the swine. The rotten, beastly swine. I could cheerfully kill him.'

Antonia returned the letter to its envelope and pressed the flap to the seal.

'This might want just a smear of glue.'

The letter was lying on Barry's plate when he got in. Rose had ripped it open at the top.

She eyed him accusingly. 'I suppose she lives in style while I count every blessed penny.'

'Not at all. I send her something to help with the child, that's all.'

'*The* child? You talk about him as if you had nothing to do with it.'

'Rosie, I'm trying to spare your feelings.'

'Thanks! It's a bit late for that.'

'All right, I should have told you. I've been sending twenty pounds on the first of each month. Michael will be starting school soon.'

'I don't want to hear about him.'

'As you wish.'

He took her at her word. She was glad of a minute or two's respite. She busied herself with the herrings she was grilling and tried to look unconcerned. She didn't speak again until she put the plate in front of him.

She said, 'What are you going to do about the bank?'

'I'll speak to Roberts. Have to go and see him, I suppose. How did he sound on the phone?'

'I've no idea. I mean I was too shocked to notice.'

'I've got a bit in National Savings. And I might be able to raise something on the insurance.'

'Where does that leave me if you drop dead?'

'What else do you suggest?'

'Why don't you pawn my wedding ring? It doesn't mean a thing to me any more.'

'This isn't like you, Rose.'

'Oh, dry up, will you?'

'Do you want a divorce?'

'So that you can clear off and marry your tart and settle all your problems? Smart

thinking, Barry. I've got to hand it to you—
you're no fool, whatever else you are. No, I
don't want a divorce. It would just about
kill my parents, and you know it. Better
think again.'

They finished the meal in silence.

Barry drew aside the bedroom curtains in
the morning about 6.30 as he always did.
There was heavy condensation on the glass
so he used the sleeve of his pyjamas to wipe
one of the panes clear.

'Bloody hell!'

Rose stirred under the bedclothes.

'What is it now?'

'Come and see.'

'It's too cold.'

His voice took on an odd, shrill note.
'I won't stand for this. It's enough to turn
your stomach. I'll get on to the council. See
if I don't. Bloody liberty. As if we haven't
got enough to put up with.'

When Barry had gone out to the bathroom, Rose slipped out of bed and went to
the window. She, too, was profoundly disturbed by what she saw. She had heard some
workmen hammering the day before and she
had assumed they were fencing off the bomb
site to keep the children from playing there.

They had erected a vast hoarding filled with the white face of a woman, a face unmistakably stricken with grief. Her pallor was set against the black hat with drapes and veil and the black high-necked dress that she wore. The lips were bloodless and the grey eyes stared upwards, focusing on nothing. The slogan under the face was 'KEEP DEATH OFF THE ROAD.' Under it, in smaller LETTERING, 'CARELESSNESS KILLS'.

6

THE next Friday afternoon about half past five Rose opened the door to a man with a bicycle pump tucked under his arm like a swagger stick. He raised his hat. The horrid poster behind him was gleaming in the lamplight, throwing him into silhouette.

'Mrs Bell?'

'Yes.'

'Smart.' As if no more was needed to be said he stooped to remove his cycle clips.

Rose held on to the door. The metal plate on their doorpost to discourage hawkers and circulars had gone in the bombing, and she was wary of being pestered. It was a nuisance having a front door that opened directly on to the street.

He stood up straight and stepped closer. 'Arnold Smart. Don't you remember?'

Faintly she did. There was something about the nasal twang in the voice.

'I call once a month to collect the premium. Your husband usually comes to the door.'

'Oh, insurance.'

'Obviously I've come at an awkward moment, but as your husband mentioned some urgency in the matter . . .'

'Is that so?'

'. . . I thought I'd drop the form in now. Isn't he at home?'

'He's always late on Fridays. I'll give him the form if you like. What is it exactly?'

He fingered his necktie. 'Might I step inside and wait? I don't wish to be a nuisance but I'd like to offer him some professional advice if I may.'

'I don't expect him until ten at the earliest.'

'Ten? That *is* rather late. I'd better come back another day. I do think a word in confidence might be advisable.'

She lost her patience. 'For heaven's sake,

what's all the mystery for? I'm his wife. He doesn't do anything without consulting me.'

'You've discussed this with him?'

'Frequently.'

'Forgive me, then. I wasn't aware of that. It's entirely up to Wing Commander Bell, of course, but I'd weigh the advantages very carefully before surrendering a policy as valuable as his.'

Alarm bells sounded in her head, but she managed to give the impression she'd heard nothing new. 'You mean cashing it in? What's wrong with that?'

'It's a lot to sacrifice for a short-term gain. You'd get only a fraction of the five thousand you would realize on maturity—or if anything should happen to him. Far be it from me to frighten you, but I'm constantly hearing of good men struck down in their prime. None of us knows what fate has in store for us.'

'I'll mention it. Perhaps we ought to think again.'

'I strongly recommend that you do. If it's a temporary difficulty you have, we could talk about a loan of equivalent value.'

'Yes, why don't you come back and talk to my husband another evening?'

'The earliest I could manage is next Thursday.'

'That would be much more convenient. Why don't you keep the surrender form until then?'

He lifted his hat again and returned to his bicycle, propped against the kerb. He fastened the pump in place, put on the clips and pedalled away, past the great, pale face of the widow.

Rose returned to the kitchen, pulled a chair from the table and said aloud, 'You bastard, Barry. You stinking rotten bastard.'

He'd meant what he said. He was about to sell off her security. If he dropped dead and she was uninsured, she would be left with nothing but his debts.

Their marriage had become a mockery long before Barry had disclosed the existence of his second family. He'd said a number of times that Rose could have a divorce, knowing, of course, that it would break the hearts of the two dear people she had left in the world to love. For her parents' sake she'd resolved to endure a loveless marriage to a faithless man. She'd made that decision when Barry had finally admitted to picking up women for sex. She'd lived with that humiliation long enough.

Now he had discovered that he couldn't keep two homes, two women and a child on his pathetic income. He proposed to surrender the insurance to pay off the overdraft. Deluded idiot. What would that achieve? The demands would only increase. The boy was growing up, starting school soon. Obviously it suited Stella Paxton to pester Barry relentlessly, destroy the marriage and take him as her husband.

Rose wanted to say, take the swine, you're welcome to him, yet there remained the sticking point. Because she would not consider a divorce whilst her parents were alive, she faced not only humiliation and hurt, but insolvency.

Since the war ended she'd suffered a steep drop in her standard of living to satisfy Barry's pride that he could support a wife. She'd made do with shapeless Utility clothes. Hadn't been to a hairdresser's. Hadn't been taken to the pictures or a dance. Her sacrifices had helped to pay the premiums on that insurance. She would have enjoyed going out to work if he hadn't made such an issue about it shaming a man. Too late now. Any money she made would go the same way as the rest.

Realistically, nothing short of Barry being killed could make any difference. Antonia had the solution—if she was serious.

An accident.

Rose admitted no inconsistency in her thinking. She had been brought up by loving parents who lived by the Ten Commandments. Any breach of Holy Law that she had committed as a child had so manifestly upset them that she had taken it to be a sin against her parents, rather than against God. She had found it very easy to forget about the God who was in Heaven. The only way to survive as a vicar's daughter was to treat your father as God. You could do anything at all so long as you kept him in blissful ignorance.

Barry had forced her hand. She had until Thursday evening if she was to get a penny of the insurance.

She was studying the calendar when she heard the key turn in the front door. She looked at the clock. It wasn't even eight yet.

Barry thrust open the kitchen door.

'Surprised you?'

'Well, yes.'

'What's up? You look peeved.'

'My eyes are sore, that's all.'

'See if these help.'

He handed her a bunch of red roses.

'Believe it or not, he expected the works.'

Antonia's eyes widened unusually. She hardly ever registered surprise. She had a way of treating everything as if she were hearing it for the second time. 'And did you let him?'

'Of course not. As if one bunch of flowers cancelled out all the women he's had.'

'The red roses must have cost him a packet.'

'I'm not one of his Friday night tarts and I told him so. I told him to take a cold bath.'

Antonia almost purred in approval. 'Nice work! Did he get nasty?'

'He went down to the pub until closing time. When he came in he made a clumsy effort to paw me so I bit his ear.'

'Darling, after what happened last time, you've got some pluck.'

'I was so angry I didn't think. He let me alone after that.'

Rose glared at a fat woman on an adjacent table who had stopped eating her blackberry flan the better to overhear what was said. They were in the marbled setting of the Strand Corner House. Any afternoon between the hours of three and four many a lapse of conduct was discussed over the silver-plated teapots. A string quartet was playing 'My dreams are getting better all the time'. Antonia was in yet another new outfit that looked as if it came from Harrods, a white pillbox hat and an emerald green two-piece with white polka dots.

'I wonder what he hoped to achieve.'

From the long look Antonia gave as she spoke it was clear that she suspected Barry of plotting something. Rose knew better. 'He's like that. He thinks all his faults are forgiven in bed. Sometimes they have been, I don't mind admitting. Well, forgotten, if not forgiven. I can't live like a nun. It's against nature. Good, she's leaving.'

The fat woman ostentatiously pushed aside her teacup and marched out.

Rose hardly paused. She was coming out with things that she wouldn't have discussed with a living soul until a few days ago. She heard herself analysing Barry's behaviour with such steely detachment that it might have been Antonia speaking. 'I suppose he could have been trying to sweeten me in case I raised Cain about the insurance, but I doubt it. Barry isn't a schemer. He lives for the moment, and that's what landed us in our present mess.'

Antonia, evidently sensing where this was

leading attempted to head Rose off with some homespun philosophy. 'Men like him won the war for us, but they can't cope in peace-time.'

'So?'

'Have some more tea.'

'Damn the tea.'

She felt entitled to some straight talking. It was obvious Antonia knew what was in her mind and was shying away from it with her platitudes about the war and her fussing with the teapot.

'What I'm telling you is that I'd be better off if Barry was dead.'

'Well, yes.' Antonia smiled and seemed to want to make light of it. 'Five thousand pounds better off.'

'Not if he signs that surrender form on Thursday.'

The point still appeared to elude Antonia. 'So you've got four days to change his mind.'

'Unless.'

'Unless what darling?'

'Unless something happens to him.'

There was an interval when nothing was said. A syrupy Viennese waltz filled the silence. Antonia pushed some hair back from her forehead and looked far across the restaurant.

'Well, Rose, my dear, you'd better say exactly what's in your mind.'

'I want him to have an accident, like you said the other day.'

There was a glint of amusement in the green eyes. 'Did I?'

'Don't tease. You know you did. Outside the Ritz.'

'And you believed me, darling?'

'For Christ's sake, Antonia, if you weren't serious, you'd better tell me, because I am.'

'An accident? Well, it's not impossible. I'd have to think about it.' She traced her fingertip around the rim of her cup. 'I suppose Barry had to give up the flying when he was demobbed?'

'He hasn't seen an airfield since the war.'

'Does he drive?'

Rose shook her head. 'We can't afford a car on his income.'

'This is difficult. Is he a swimmer?'

'I'm afraid not. That is to say, I believe he *can* swim, but he doesn't ever go near water. He's not the athletic type.'

'Is he the handyman type? Could he be persuaded to replace those missing tiles on your roof?'

Desperate as she felt, Rose couldn't suppress a smile. 'Good idea, but definitely not. He absolutely refuses.'

'We're not getting very far, are we? Suppose we go about this another way. You tell me everything he does from the moment he gets up in the morning.'

'In detail?'

'The more the better.'

'I'll try.' Rose closed her eyes and concentrated. 'Wakes up at 6.30 when the alarm goes. Groans. Heaves himself out and reaches for his slippers. Shuffles into the bathroom and uses the toilet. You asked for everything.'

'I meant it. Don't stop now.'

'Goes to the washbasin and runs the hot tap. Swears when it comes out almost cold. Swishes some over his face. Makes a lather for a shave.'

'What sort of razor?'

'Safety, I'm afraid. Brushes his teeth.'

'Toothpowder?'

'Paste. Returns to the bedroom and dresses. Woollen underwear. Blue pinstripe. White shirt and collar. Any one of three striped ties. Meanwhile, I've slipped downstairs in my dressing-gown and cooked some porridge and made toast. He comes down and opens the Ideal boiler and empties the ashcan. This is frightfully boring.'

'I'm hanging on every word.'

So Rose picked her way patiently through the daily routine until she had got Barry into bed again and switched out the light. 'Well?'

'His journey home. Go through it again.'

'But I've told you it's as safe as houses. The Stationery Office depot is just behind Harvey Nichols, so he walks around the corner to Knightsbridge tube station and gets a Piccadilly Line train to South Ken. He changes to the District Line and comes back to Victoria and walks it from there, straight down St George's Drive. He's home by a quarter past six, except for Fridays. He switches on the wireless and hears the last part of the news.'

'What time does he leave work?'

'Half past five.'

'Carrying his briefcase and umbrella?'

Rose gripped the edge of the table and leaned forward. 'Have you thought of something?'

Some seconds passed before Antonia spoke. 'Let's get one thing straight, my flower. Did you mean every word you said about Barry? You really want him to have an accident?'

7

ON Wednesday afternoons the Imperial College timetable was marked 'Sport'. Some of the staff unselfishly turned out to referee football matches or cycle along the towpath shouting through megaphones. Vic went to bed with Antonia.

If it counted as sport it was of championship quality, brilliantly performed. He managed to be tender and passionate just as desired, alert to every signal she gave. She cried out repeatedly and gritted her teeth and promised herself she would never be parted from him. It was impossible to imagine it with anyone else.

The climax left every sport for dead. It should have been set to music and played at the last night of the proms. Then they lay still.

Presently he pressed his hands into the pillow and eased himself upwards to get a better sight of her. 'These are pretty terrific, too.'

'I'll settle for pretty.'

'Just pretty, then.' He continued to look.

'Cover me up for the love of Mike. There's a wicked draught coming in.'

He removed his weight and Antonia gripped the bedclothes and pulled them up to her neck. Vic found enough space to lie on his side, resting his hand on the flat of her stomach. She let it remain there.

'I didn't know you were cold.'

'I was coming out in goosepimples.'

'Is that what they were?'

'Ha bloody ha.'

'Want a fag?'

'All right.'

They lit up. She waited a while before asking what she was dying to know.

'Have you heard any more from America?'

'No.'

'Is it still on?'

'I'm afraid so. Can't we talk about something else?'

'If you wish. What would you say to getting married next spring?'

He twisted around to face her and almost fell out of bed in the process. He grabbed her arm. 'What?'

'You heard, lover.'

'You're not free to marry anyone.'

'I might be if I get a good offer.'

'How come? What about Hector? I thought divorce was out of the question.'

'Vic, just answer my question, will you? Would you marry me if I was free?'

'Christ, I never thought of it as a possibility.'

'We love each other, don't we?'

'Well, yes. But I don't see how—'

She put a finger against his lips. 'Yes, or no?'

The puzzled look remained.

'Vic, I want an answer.'

'Yes, then.'

'Good. I don't consider this a proposal, by the way. You can save that up for the appropriate time.'

'When's that likely to be?'

'Not long.'

By Thursday Antonia had twice travelled the tube with Barry. She had waited for the evening exodus of bowler-hatted civil servants from the Stationery Office depot at 5.30. She'd taken the precaution of concealing her hair in a headscarf knotted at the front, factory-girl style, and she wasn't wearing lipstick. She had kept her distance when Barry crossed Sloane Street and made a beeline for the tube station, but she needn't actually have bothered because he hadn't been looking about him. He'd had that faraway expression that you see on the face of regular travellers. Anyway, it was six years or more since she'd been to bed with him.

Those six years had taken their toll of Barry. The laughlines were deep creases now and his neck had thickened and was chafed by a collar that he'd obviously outgrown. He'd kept the handlebar moustache and, if anything, it was bushier than before, only it simply didn't go with the bowler hat; he should have shaved it off on the day he was demobbed. Perhaps it wasn't fair to draw conclusions from someone's appearance after a day at the office, yet it seemed to Antonia that Barry had looked more jaded than he had in the old days after many nights of flying. She had no difficulty picturing him among the middle-aged men in hotel bars on Friday evenings who leered optimistically at anything in skirts.

Still, an ex-pilot's reactions ought to be sharper than the average man's. Better not underestimate him.

She had watched him buy his evening paper from the man at the underground entrance. He'd studied the front page all the way down the escalator, so she had been able to get really close to him. It was worth the risk because she could easily have lost him in the rush for the platform when the rumble of a train was heard.

Barry had evidently worked out the most convenient point at which to board the train. It suited him best to be at the rear, which meant walking the length of the platform to the Brompton Road end, behind the people waiting three and four deep. Each of the two evenings she had observed him he had allowed one train to draw in and leave, making no attempt to get on board. This way he guaranteed himself a front position at the edge of the platform. And a seat on the next train.

The position he took up was some twenty yards from the tunnel. The trains came in so fast that they couldn't possibly halt until they were more than halfway along the platform.

It wouldn't be a lingering death.

And now it was Friday and she was already on the platform, standing by a chocolate machine. She'd decided there was no need to follow him all the way down the escalator. She could wait here in confidence that he'd shortly be along. This time she had put on a plain blue and white headscarf knotted under the neck like most of the shopgirls and typists standing around her. She had a light brown coat with a belt and she was wearing gloves and flat shoes. She had an empty handbag looped over her arm.

She glanced at the clock overhead. Time enough. He should appear in two or three minutes. Two Uxbridge-bound trains had already come in, filled and gone. The platform didn't empty between trains, so she wasn't conspicuous among the numbers still waiting. Some people stood back anyway, wanting Hounslow trains.

Presently came the drone of another, building steadily in volume. The power of the tube thrilled Antonia when she had first experienced it at four years old. She'd found it vastly more exciting than the West End pantomime she was being taken to see. Even as an adult she preferred it to the buses.

Sparks lit the interior of the tunnel. She mentally rehearsed while the front of the train filled the void and thundered towards her. She saw the driver, picked out by the station lights, pale, staring ahead, his hands on the controls. The push would have to be perfectly timed and forceful.

One good shove.

A mass of red crossed her vision. The

train came to a screeching stop and the doors opened. Suppose, after all, he sees a space and gets on at the other end, she thought, then told herself it wasn't possible. Barry had his routine. She just had to keep her nerve.

The sliding doors stuttered and closed and that train moved out.

The forward move to claim front positions along the platform edge had begun again. Barry still hadn't arrived. Antonia looked up at the clock and stared towards the far end.

She watched the train depart until the last spark in the tunnel, then shifted her gaze to the oncoming passengers, mentally sorting bowler hats from trilbies and checking for large moustaches.

She spotted him.

He was walking towards her in his black raincoat and carrying his scuffed leather briefcase in one hand and his newspaper in the other, with the umbrella hanging over his arm. He stared blankly ahead.

Antonia put her hand to her face as if to yawn and turned towards the map of the underground behind her. She could still watch Barry's approach. He stopped barely five yards from her.

The faint hum of the next train increased

in resonance to a braying note. People stood four or five deep the length of the platform. Barry turned his paper over to look at the sport. He would let this one go.

In it rushed. The ranks broke and converged on the doors. An announcer appealed to people to stand back and let the passengers off first. Barry folded his paper and tucked it away in his briefcase.

The doors parted, people stepped out and others surged forward to take their places. The voice on the loudspeaker system sounded shocked at the mayhem.

'There'll be another one along in a minute.'

Barry was becoming restless, looking about him to see who else was in contention for a seat on the next train. Antonia put her hand to her face again.

'Stand back, please.'

The doors closed. Barry and scores of others stepped forward and formed the front rank before the train moved off. Antonia coolly advanced a couple of steps. She didn't join the line yet. She would go closer when the moment was right.

Her concentration was total. The ability to blot out what she called distractions had always been one of her strengths. During the Battle of Britain air raids she had surprised everyone who took her to be skittish and unstable by her utter reliability plotting the movement of aircraft. At this minute Barry was as impersonal to her as the metal arrows she had prodded across the map.

More passengers kept streaming in from both ends of the platform. The next train was signalled. She heard it faintly. The congestion at the platform edge increased. She moved decisively and stood behind Barry, so close that she couldn't any longer see the advertisements on the opposite wall. She had a view instead of a small section of the track, glimpsed between Barry's leg and the next man's. She could see the four rails Hector had painstakingly described for her. And the pit below the rails.

She was conscious of people closing up behind her, someone tall. She didn't turn round to look. She had a middle-aged woman on her right and a soldier on her left.

This would all be in the timing. She listened acutely to the drone coming from the tunnel, heard the swishing sound made by the sparks. She had to judge everything on the sound.

Any second.

Barry's back was beautifully straight, his legs very slightly apart.

Her eardrums throbbed to the train's roar.
Now.

She took a half step backwards and leaned into the man behind her. The moment she felt her back in contact with him she turned her head and said loudly, 'Stop pushing, will you?'

At the same time she thrust both hands hard into the small of Barry's back.

He tipped over the edge like a skittle just as the train rushed from the tunnel.

Antonia's scream merged with the screech of the brakes. Just as she'd estimated, the train travelled most of the way along the platform before it stopped. This time the doors didn't open. Other women were screaming now.

She said, 'Oh, God, we've got to get help!' and pushed her way past the woman beside her, through the crowd and out of the exit tunnel.

In a moment she glanced behind. Nobody had followed her. She took off her headscarf and walked to the escalator.

8

Rose snatched up the receiver the moment it rang.

Antonia sounded like a telephone operator, friendly and businesslike at the same time.

'Darling, are you alone?'

'Yes.'

'Been at home all morning?'

'Yes, of course. Did you . . . ?'

'Try and look surprised when they break the news to you. I'll call you in a few days.'

The phone clicked and purred.

Rose hung up. She reached for her handbag. Smelling-salts. Couldn't faint now. Unscrewed the stopper and held it to her nose. This must be a dream. Everything up to now is a dream.

They took her to the mortuary in a police car and showed her Barry's body. More precisely, they showed her his face. She braced herself for a harrowing sight, yet he was not at all disfigured. Even the moustache was intact and reasonably tidy. He was so different from her expectation, so unmarked, that she had a horrid feeling he would open his eyes when she identified him. She nodded her head and turned away. It was no longer a dream.

They assured her that he must have been electrocuted before the train hit him. Six hundred volts had stopped his heart immediately so he hadn't known much about it. On what authority they had reached this conclusion they didn't specify. Anything was justifiable to comfort the bereaved, she supposed. They said nothing about the state of his injuries under the green canvas covering. All that they kept repeating was that he hadn't suffered. She heard herself say thank you, as if *they* had arranged it humanely. The sergeant put his hands on her shoulders and steered her outside. She wept in the car as they drove her back to Oldfield Gardens. She was weeping for herself and her fear of what would happen. The sergeant said a cry would do her good.

She stood in her doorway and watched the police car drive away. Before she closed the door she glanced across at the poster of the widow. Someone had drawn a large tear under one of the eyes and scrawled 'sperlash!' underneath.

Alone in the house, she started to shiver. She opened the boiler to let it draw, knowing really that cold wasn't the cause. The anthracite Barry had tipped in after breakfast was still burning.

They had told her there would have to be a post mortem and an inquest. She wouldn't be required to say much, if anything.

She felt numb. She thought of what she had said to Antonia. *'I want him to have an accident.'* A death sentence.

I condemned my own husband to death and asked someone else to be the executioner. Was that really what I intended? Wasn't it just a cry of despair that Antonia misunderstood?

No, I can't duck the truth. I meant what I said. I wanted him removed and she was willing to do it. We called it an accident and it sounded excusable. We didn't describe it as a killing. Or murder.

It was an accident. I've got to think of it as an accident, or how will I convince everyone else?

She got up and tried to occupy herself by taking the carpet sweeper into the front room and using it until her arms ached. On the table was the vase containing the roses Barry had brought home for her the previous Friday. They had darkened and drooped. After she'd carried them to the boiler she noticed blood on her fingers. She'd gripped the stems so tightly that she hadn't felt the thorn pierce her skin. And she'd left a trail of red petals across the floor. She reached for the carpet sweeper again.

She needed distraction and nothing she did would supply it. Several times she considered ringing her mother, then couldn't brace herself to tell the lies that would be necessary. Later, perhaps.

Increasingly she grew fearful of the truth coming out. There was going to be an inquest. The coroner would try to discover what actually had happened in the underground. There would be witnesses.

It troubled Rose that she had practically no knowledge of what had happened on Knightsbridge Station. Antonia had given her no clue. She might have bungled it terribly. There might be witnesses who would swear they had seen a woman push Barry off the platform. They could provide descriptions. Someone could have followed Antonia after Barry fell. At this very minute she might be making a statement to the police.

Rose was in no doubt that if Antonia was caught and accused, she'd name her accomplice.

She opened the larder and reached for the brandy and just at that moment the doorbell rang. The brandy bottle slipped from her grasp and smashed on the floor. She was petrified.

By now it was past eight. All the lights were on. She couldn't pretend she was out.

It rang again, longer, more insistently.

She sighed heavily, stepped over the mess the broken bottle had made and went with mechanical steps through the passage to see who was at the door.

The light wasn't helpful. That wretched poster threw everything in front of it into shadow. Momentarily she believed she saw a policeman with drawn truncheon standing on the doorstep. Then she realized it was a bicycle pump he was holding.

Mr Smart, the insurance agent. He'd arranged to come back with the surrender form. He gave a professional smile.

'Sorry to be calling so late, Mrs Bell. I tried earlier, but you were both out, so I came back. Is your husband at home?'

'He's dead.'

The smile vanished. 'Dead?'

'This afternoon.'

'You're serious? Quite, quite, quite. I can see you are. Oh, my word. How appalling.'

'Yes.'

'Dreadful. Might I enquire . . . ?'

'An accident.'

'On the road?'

'In the tube.'

'The tube? He didn't . . .'

'. . . take his own life? Apparently not. They told me it was an accident. He fell off the platform.'

'Poor fellow. Poor you, Mrs Bell. Tripped and fell. Pardon me for asking, but approximately what time did the tragedy occur?'

'Between 5.30 and six, I suppose. I didn't ask.'

'And at which station, Mrs Bell? The reason I enquire is that in certain cases, very occasionally I hasten to say, the company appoints investigators. Most unlikely in this case, I should think.'

'It was Knightsbridge.'

'Ah. The District Line?'

'The Piccadilly.'

'Yes, of course. Impossibly overcrowded

at that time. I say, are you alone? Isn't there anyone with you?'

'I'd rather be left to myself, thank you.'

'You're quite sure there's nothing I can do? Rest assured that the company will fulfil its obligations to the letter. To the letter, Mrs Bell. I presume there will have to be an inquest. We are obliged to wait until after that, you understand. Forgive me for saying so, but how providential that your husband didn't surrender his policy when I called last week. God moves in mysterious ways, doesn't He? Then if you're absolutely certain I can't be of any practical help . . .'

He backed away as if he couldn't wait to escape, for all his professions of concern. In seconds he was pedalling his bike so fast up the street that his dynamo lamp put out a beam like a searchlight.

Several more times in the next few days Rose's nerves were tested by unexpected callers. Each time she expected to be arrested. The vicar called on Friday and recommended talking to God as a remedy for grief. On Saturday morning two men in raincoats looked so like detectives that she actually did send up a prayer. They turned out to be colleagues of Barry's from the Stationery

Office, calling to express their condolences. She made some coffee and they all said that Barry was a fine man struck down in his prime. The same morning one of the neighbours called and asked her to sign a petition to have the hoarding across the street removed. When she saw the sheet of paper in his hand she thought it was a summons.

By degrees she started to believe that her arrest was not, after all, imminent. She busied herself writing to everyone who needed to know about Barry's passing. He hadn't made a will, so she asked the bank for legal advice and they offered the services of their legal department. She phoned her parents after Evensong on Sunday. They wanted her to leave everything and come to the Rectory, but she said she preferred to stay busy, and there was plenty to occupy her in Pimlico.

Daddy asked if she had some friend she could rely on to help her through this ordeal. She answered yes and thought of Antonia. She couldn't have faced it without.

Hector was listening to the *Brains Trust*. He habitually tuned in on Sunday afternoons at four. He didn't listen much to the wireless, except for the news, preferring to spend his evenings working upstairs in his office. He found comedy programmes like *ITMA*, which always had Antonia shrieking with laughter, impossible to follow. But Professor Joad and the others talked good sense at a speed he could understand.

To his surprise, Antonia had joined him in the drawing room beside the set. She'd arrived midway through with tea on a tray, which he was afraid would bring his listening to a premature end, but she sat in silence until he switched off at the end.

She asked, 'Was it as riveting as usual?'

'Better than last week. Better questions.'

'Let's have a *Brains Trust* of our own. I've got a question for you.'

'Yes?'

'What would you do if I was dead?'

He sniffed. 'Funny question.'

'On the contrary, my swain, it's serious. I can hardly wait to hear your answer. Suppose I hopped the twig. Would you be able to manage without me?'

He gave her a pained stare. 'Why do you ask me such a ghastly thing?'

'Be honest, Hec. You'd be a free man again. No one to tear strips off you when you came in late. No enormous bills from

Harrods and Fortnums at the end of each month. You could live the life of Riley.'

Hector's logical mind hadn't got past her first proposition. 'You are not ill?'

'God, no.'

'You wouldn't kill yourself? That time we talked about the tube, it was a joke?'

She felt the colour rise to her face. 'The tube? A joke, yes—forget about that. Dismiss it from your mind. I already have.'

'Then I don't understand the question.'

'It's hypothetical.'

'Sometimes, Antonia, I find you impossible to understand.'

9

ROSE's thoughts couldn't stretch beyond the inquest. She dreaded having to appear in public, trying to seem convincing as the devoted widow in front of all those experts and professionals. The letter arrived on Monday, a stiffly worded notice from the coroner's office asking her to attend the court on Thursday at 11 a.m. It terrified her. On Wednesday night she had the worst nightmares of her life.

Mr Burden, one of the senior people from

the depot where Barry had worked, decently arranged to collect her in a taxi and accompany her to the court. He was an overbearing man who talked nonstop about Barry and what marvellous company he'd been with his saucy stories and witty remarks. Rose looked out of the window.

It turned out to be unlike anything she had expected. Barry's was only one of a series of deaths that were up for consideration. The case wasn't called until nearly noon. Inside there were no wigs or robes to be seen and the coroner looked and sounded like a variety turn. He could easily have passed for one of the Western brothers, such was his air of suave, world-weary irony.

Rose was more alarmed than reassured. When the main witness, Albert Abbot, a street vendor, was called there was a question about the goods he sold. Abbot insisted on using the term 'haberdashery' and the coroner said he presumed the witness meant nylons on the black market. The comment was mean considering that there were police witnesses present. Abbot was obviously used to looking after himself and he wouldn't be drawn, but Rose knew that when her turn came she was most unlikely to get away with any evasions.

Abbot's evidence was crucial. He had been on Knightsbridge Station standing close to Barry on the evening he was killed.

'I was taking the tube to Earls Court like I always do round about that time.'

'What time, Mr Abbot—or is that something else you wish to conceal?'

'Quarter to six, and I've got nothing to conceal. I seen him regular down there. Handlebars out to here. Couldn't miss him, could I? Always got himself a seat in the end carriage. When the train come in he was through them doors like a jackrabbit.'

'But not on the evening in question.'

'That's obvious, isn't it?'

'I am endeavouring to establish what you saw on that occasion, Mr Abbot.'

'Right. When I come along, he was in his usual spot, nicely placed for the doors. He'd worked out the right place to stand, right opposite the Sandeman poster. As a matter of fact, I always made a point of getting as close to him as I could.'

'Because you assumed he was likely to be one of the first aboard the train?'

'Didn't I say that? I like to get into the train quick, so I can stand my suitcase containing my haberdashery just inside the doors where people won't fall over it. It's a fair size, that case. All right, your honour, I'm coming to it. Upon the evening in question, to use your words, I wasn't quick enough to get right behind him. Some doll steps in first.'

Rose twisted two fingers in the strap of her handbag and tightened them. She was beside Mr Burden, three rows from the front. She'd borrowed a black coat for the inquest and found a small matching hat to which she had sewn stiffened net to veil the upper part of her face. It made her conspicuous, but she couldn't risk giving the impression that she was anything but griefstricken.

'If this is the young lady who featured in the fatal incident, you will need to furnish a better description than "some doll", Mr Abbot.'

'Right you are, your honour. She was quite tall, dark coat, brown, I think, with a belt. She was wearing a scarf on her head, so I don't know what colour hair she had. I didn't see much of her face either, but you can take it from me she was twenty-five or thereabouts. Nine times out of ten you can tell from the back.'

There was some subdued amusement at this.

'What I or anyone else can tell from the

back is of no consequence, Mr Abbot. It is your assessment that matters, and if you tell us that the young lady was twenty-five, so be it. At this point I should inform the members of the jury that despite extensive enquiries by the police, they have been unable as yet to trace the person just described.'

Rose swallowed and looked straight ahead.

'Kindly continue, Mr Abbot.'

'Well, like I said, she was standing behind the bloke with the handlebars, and I was right behind her. To be honest, it's always a bit of a scrum when the train starts coming. She sort of took a step back when I was about to move forward. I got an elbow in my ribs and she half turned round and yelled at me to stop pushing.'

'And were you?'

'Strewth, no. I say that on my word of honour.'

'I hope everything you have told us is on your word of honour, Mr Abbot. It had better not be otherwise. What happened after she complained?'

'She seemed to lose her balance. She put out her hands and gave the poor beggar a shove in the back. He was taken by surprise and what with his briefcase and umbrella he couldn't do nothing to save himself. The train was just coming in and he fell straight in front of it. He must have been killed outright. He didn't suffer.'

'Thank you for your reassurance on that point. However, we'll hear the opinion of our medical witness before reaching a conclusion.'

'Just as you like. I was there.'

'That is not in dispute. And did you notice the young woman's reaction to the incident?'

'She had her back to me, like I said. She screamed. She said something about getting some help. Then she pushed past the woman next to her and I didn't see where she went after that. There was women screaming and some people running away and others wanting to have a look.'

'You are quite certain that she said she was going for help? There is no evidence that she stopped to report the incident to anyone.'

'She must have panicked and run off.'

The coroner was letting nothing get by. 'You're not here to give an opinion, Mr Abbot. Do you remember precisely what she said after she stopped screaming?'

'Not every word, no. I was trying to see

what happened to the poor bloke under the train, wasn't I?'

'However, the gist of what she said was that she intended to go for assistance?'

'For help, yes.'

'I think there is no purpose in persisting with this. Unless the jury have any questions they wish to put to the witness, he may stand down. Thank you, Mr Abbot.'

A second witness, a soldier, gave evidence next and added nothing to Abbot's version of events. He was questioned closely about what he had observed of the fatal push. He had seen the woman in the headscarf sway back and forward and he was satisfied that she had reached out because she had lost her balance.

A London Transport official described the procedure for getting the public safely aboard trains in the rush-hour. It was agreed that Knightsbridge was one of the busiest stations, with passengers streaming in from either end of the platform. However this was the first time such an incident had occurred there. The edge of the platform was paved with ribbed stones to prevent people slipping and most people stood back a yard or so until the train stopped.

The coroner asked whether it was reasonable for someone to take a step back-wards when the train came in.

'Somebody standing close to the tunnel might. You get a gust of air as well as the sound of the train.'

'But most people stand their ground?'

'Experienced travellers, yes.'

A pathologist from St George's Hospital took the stand and reported on the post mortem examination. In spite of what had been suggested, he said that death was not caused by electrocution. The impact of the train was the primary cause. The deceased had suffered multiple injuries, including a fracture to the cervical region of the vertebral column. Death had been almost instantaneous.

The coroner glanced up at the clock. 'In view of the evidence already given, I don't think it will be necessary to call Mrs Bell, the widow of the deceased, to give evidence. This might have been pertinent if there had been any possibility that the deceased took his own life, but it is evident that we can rule out suicide entirely. For the same reason I shall not be calling his employer or his doctor. I thank them for attending the court.'

Rose closed her eyes and felt the tension drain from her muscles. The relief was profound. It was a reprieve. In the state she was in she'd have given herself away, she was certain.

'Ladies and gentlemen of the jury, I shall presently ask you to reach a decision as to the probable cause of this man's unfortunate death. The sequence of events leading up to the fatal incident is not in dispute. He took up a position at the edge of the platform close to the tunnel from which the train arrived. There was some movement behind him precisely as the train was about to enter the station. The young woman immediately to his rear appeared to lose her balance and press her hands against the back of the deceased, who plunged off the platform. The train struck him and killed him. It is a matter of regret that the police have been unable to trace the lady concerned. It would have been helpful to have heard her account of the incident.'

He paused and looked around the court.

Rose sat still and looked back at him. Her veil was trembling like a web in the wind.

The coroner resumed. 'One might postulate a number of explanations, one of which I am bound to invite you to consider, however remote it may appear. If the young woman felt some malice towards the deceased, it is not impossible that she could have followed him to the station with the intention of causing his death.

'Should you feel that this hypothesis has any relevance whatsoever, I must advise you to bring in an open verdict, there being insufficient evidence to reach any stronger conclusion. I would then instruct the police to redouble their efforts to trace the woman. If, on the other hand, you take the view that there was no malice involved, then there can be no other verdict than accidental death.'

Rose looked across at the jury. They didn't even retire to consider the verdict. The foreman conferred with them and stood up.

'We believe it was an accident, sir.'

10

A sleek white Bentley Mark VI drew in smoothly to the kerb in front of St James-The-Less Church in Moreton Street where Rose had been waiting almost twenty minutes. Antonia was at the wheel.

'Hop in, darling. We're about to go slumming across the river. A pint and a pork pie in the Prince Regent. Do you know it?'

Rose didn't know it. Nor did she know

the man sitting beside Antonia. His presence threw her into angry confusion. Her first impulse was to turn and march away, and ten days ago she wouldn't have hesitated. Having it brought home to her that she was now incapable of such a simple act of independence incensed her even more as she got into the back seat. The man turned and grinned at her in a way that was meant to be friendly. He got a cold stare in return. She was in no frame of mind to be sociable. Antonia was the bloody limit. This wasn't meant to be a pub-crawl with some fancy man in tow. It was her first chance to talk to Antonia after the hellish week she'd been through.

Talk? Rose didn't trust herself to speak.

The car had turned and started across Vauxhall Bridge before she could bring herself to take another look at the man, and then her thoughts weren't charitable. Probably about her own age, he had the sort of fine black hair that would start receding before he was thirty. The deep-set brown eyes and tanned skin made her think of Italian prisoners of war in work-parties she had seen from the windows of trains. She'd always ignored their waving and whistling.

Meanwhile Antonia carried on as if it was a party. 'Say hello to Vic, darling. He's the dishiest man in London, as you can see, and I've been dying for you two to meet.'

He turned and offered his hand. It was broad, with strong-looking fingers and a crop of dark hair. Rose put hers out mechanically and had it gripped.

'Poor Rosie lost her hubby last week. A frightful accident in the tube. She's had a basinful of sympathy, so you needn't say a word.'

In Rose's estimation Vic didn't look as if comforting words were on the tip of his tongue.

She said, 'I don't want to go into a pub.'

'Nonsense, darling. A drink will do you the world of good.'

The lunch-hour was noisily in session in the Prince Regent. People stood face to face bellowing at each other. They were three-deep at the bar and there was so much smoke you could have taken it for the gun deck of a man-of-war. Why Antonia had suggested this as a place to talk was beyond Rose's compre-hension.

Vic took their orders and joined the throng at the bar.

'He'll be ages. How are you coping?'

'Can't we go somewhere more private?'

'Nobody's listening. Now it's all over

you've got to return to the world of the living.'

'Barry isn't buried yet.'

'I know that, love. You've got to pick up the death certificate, correct? We'll do it this afternoon.'

'Both of us?'

'You want some moral support, don't you?'

'Is it wise?'

'Calm down, Rose. It's perfectly normal for someone else to tag along, a friend to hold your hand, so to speak. When's the funeral?'

'The day after tomorrow.'

'We'll have a couple of drinks with Vic and I'll drive you over to the registry office. Have you filled in the insurance claim yet?'

'The bank are looking after that for me.'

'You bet they are, the sharks. Remember that's *your* money. Don't let them do you for a single penny.'

Antonia was wagging her forefinger like a schoolmistress. She finished by tapping the back of Rose's hand. Then she grasped her wrist and squeezed it.

'We pulled it off, my flower!'

Vic had cleverly succeeded in getting served at once and was edging through with a tray of drinks and slices of pie. Antonia waved her white kid gloves.

'He's divine, isn't he?'

'Who is he exactly?'

'Ask him. He isn't dumb. God, and we haven't even found a table yet.'

They had to make do with a windowsill. Vic noticed that someone had dropped cigarette ash on Rose's sleeve. He insisted on flicking it off with his handkerchief. In other circumstances she would probably have accepted him as a pleasant addition to the company. There was nothing she could object to in his behaviour. It wasn't his fault that he happened to be unwelcome. Antonia, the real culprit, bulldozed on regardless.

'Victor, my love, Rosie wants to know who the bloody hell you are.'

He gave Rose a tolerant smile. 'Don't let her bother you. She does it to me all the time. She's probably told you already, but if it's of any interest I lecture in chemistry at Imperial College.'

This wasn't enough for Antonia. 'Come on, you do research as well. You've got your own lab filled with the most fearful-looking chemicals.' She swung back to Rose. 'He could poison the whole of London if he wanted to.'

Vic rolled his eyes. 'Now why should I want to do that?'

'Tell Rose about your swimming, then. This is really bizarre, darling.'

He sighed. 'Do I have to? I'm one of that eccentric band of health fanatics who swim in the Serpentine every day. I might as well tell you the rest, or she'll make me sound like a monster. I have a liking for French films, traditional jazz and, against my better judgement, one deplorably outspoken blonde lady.'

Antonia punched him playfully in the ribs. 'You mean sophisticated, ducky.'

'I mean exactly what I said.'

His manner towards her suggested a close relationship. Rose wondered how much Antonia's husband knew about it.

Antonia gave her a nudge. 'Now it's your turn, darling.'

Rose shook her head. 'Anyone can see what I am: totally out of place in this atmosphere.'

'Rubbish. Victor, you beast, I'm going to tell you something quite remarkable about my friend Rosie: she's never comfortable with what she's wearing. For God's sake tell her she looks wonderfully elegant in black or she won't let us stay for another drink.'

Rose sighed and turned up her eyes in exasperation. 'I don't mind waiting outside.'

However she stayed and was persuaded to try some vodka in her tomato juice. Vic secured a table for them and handed round Balkan Sobranie cigarettes. Rose hadn't tried the brand before and found it strong. To mask the taste she finished her drink in a couple of gulps and Vic fetched her another. To her immense relief the focus of conversation shifted away from her. Antonia brought it round to female film stars and held forth about passive, wishy-washy heroines who deserved to be knocked about by sadists like James Mason in *The Man in Grey*. She said any intelligent woman would have stood up and applauded the scene in *The Seventh Veil* when Mason crushed Ann Todd's delicate hands under the piano lid.

Rose said she hadn't seen the films and anyway violent men had no appeal for her.

'Sorry, my poppet. Shouldn't have brought it up.'

Vic looked at his watch and remembered he had a lecture to give at two. They drove back across the river and put him off at Victoria, where he could get the tube.

Antonia blew him a kiss before he disappeared. 'Isn't he bliss to be with? I knew you'd get on famously with him.'

'That isn't the point. We had things to discuss.'

'Rosie, my precious lamb, you'd better get one thing clear in your head. Post mortems don't appeal to me in the least. I did what you asked me to do and now it's up to you to make the best of it.'

'Well, yes. Don't think I'm ungrateful, but—'

'It's beginning to sound like it.'

Rose gave up protesting. She'd allowed her emotions to dictate to her. She had craved some human contact after the ordeal of the inquest. And the one person in the world she could share her experience with had put up the shutters. Well, perhaps it was sensible. After all, there was nothing of practical importance to be discussed with Antonia. And aside from their reminiscing about the war and their bouts of giggling they hadn't truly found much in common. Antonia's brashness was a strong disincentive.

Besides, she would never be able to think of Antonia in the same way, knowing what she had done down there in the tube. Rose told herself that she personally was just as culpable—if not more so—for suggesting it. Yet she would have been incapable of pushing Barry under the train. She was convinced of that. The fact that Antonia had done it in cold blood set her apart. She was uncomfortable to be with now.

Rose said, 'You're absolutely right. I must be more self-reliant. You don't need to come with me this afternoon. Just drop me outside the registry office.'

'Darling, I'll do no such thing.'

'I mean it.'

'Shut up and listen to me. I won't be coming in just to hold your hand. You're going to help *me* this afternoon.'

'Help you? How?'

'You don't object, do you?'

Rose hesitated. 'What am I supposed to do?'

'Because it wouldn't show much gratitude, would it, little sister, after I put my precious life at risk to get you out of your particular pickle?'

'Antonia, I've said how grateful I am.'

'And now you have an opportunity to show it.'

'Tell me what you want me to do.'

Antonia drove on for some time without answering.

Rose said, 'So long as it isn't against the law.'

Antonia laughed. 'Sweetie, asking to visit the ladies isn't illegal.'

The fire in the waiting room had gone out, probably days ago. The windows were still painted over for the blackout and last summer's flypapers hung from the lights. Torn pages from *John Bull* and *Everybody's* littered the threadbare lino. About twenty people sat and stood in silence broken only by a crying child and regular coughing.

Between them, Rose and Antonia got through a packet of ten Senior Service before their turn came. They'd been told that Deaths were upstairs.

'Next.'

'You know what to say?' said Antonia before they went in. 'You're looking awfully pale.'

'Isn't that the idea?'

The Assistant Registrar (Deaths) Knock Before Entering had a purple twinset that tended to emphasize the papery appearance of her skin. Her coke stove was alight and the clock on the wall was ticking. She was writing the date on the top sheet of her pad of death certificates.

'Yes?'

Antonia steered Rose forward by the arm, as if she were blind. 'This is Mrs Bell, whose husband was unfortunately taken from her in an accident last week. I'm her friend.'

'Is she the informant, or are you?'

'She is.'

'Can't she speak for herself?'

'She's rather distressed.'

Rose smiled wanly at Antonia. 'I'll try.'

'The name of the deceased, then?'

'Bell. Barry Desborough Bell, DFC. Wing Commander.'

'So his occupation was RAF Officer?'

'No. Civil Servant. Clerical Officer.'

'So you mean Wing Commander retired. You should have said so. I could have spoilt the certificate, couldn't I? What was the date of death?'

'October 10th.'

'As long ago as that?'

'There was an inquest.'

'I see. I can't do anything without a report from the coroner, you know.'

'His office said it would be here this morning.'

'They promise all sorts of things. Fill in this form, please. This is not the death certificate, but one we require for our records.'

The registrar snatched up a sheaf of papers from her in-tray and thumbed rapidly through them. Rose dipped the pen in the ink and started to write, prompted once or twice by Antonia.

'*Your* name.'

'Oh, yes.'

Suddenly Rose put down the pen and turned to Antonia. 'I think I'm going to be sick.'

The registrar scraped back her chair. For a moment it seemed that she meant to escort Rose to the toilet. Apparently she thought better of it.

'Downstairs and to the right at the foot of the staircase. Second door.'

Antonia got up and opened the door. 'Do you want me to come?' She mouthed the words, 'Say you can't find it.'

'I can manage. It may be just a drink of water I need.'

Rose went out. The registrar started again on her sheaf of papers, watched by Antonia. The tick of the clock was like a time-bomb.

The door opened again and Rose looked in. 'I'm fearfully sorry.'

The registrar stared at her. 'What's happened? Didn't you reach it in time?'

105

'I couldn't find it. Could I trouble you to show me?'

With a sigh like a burner in a balloon, the registrar rose, yanked her cardigan across her chest and stumped to the door. 'It's perfectly easy to find.' Halfway downstairs she turned and asked Rose if she was pregnant.

Somehow, Rose held herself in check. She was sorely tempted to ask the same question back. However, she'd agreed to go through with this, so she shook her head and followed meekly down the rest of the stairs to the appropriate room.

At least the woman had the grace to tell her to take her time, although possibly her office floor was paramount in her thoughts.

Rose whiled away some minutes studying the walls. She'd never understood what drove people to publicize their love and hate in such places. Then she washed and dried her hands and returned upstairs. Antonia sprang up and grasped her hand and asked if she felt any better. It seemed like over-acting, though the registrar ignored the performance. She announced that she had located the letter from the coroner's office. The paperwork was completed in a short time. Rose paid the fee for extra copies of the death certificate and put the documents in her handbag.

Outside in the Bentley, Antonia leaned across and planted a loud kiss on Rose's cheek.

'You were brilliant, darling. Brilliant! It was quite a blow when she didn't go out with you the first time. What an old dragon!'

'Are you going to tell me what it was all about?'

'Haven't you guessed by now? Look.'

Antonia opened her handbag and took out a folded piece of paper. She spread it across her knees and then passed it to Rose.

'A death certificate?'

'A *blank* death certificate—with the duplicate they keep for their records.'

'You took it from her desk? But it's got a number on it. She'll know it's missing.'

'She won't. I'm not soft in the head, Rosie, my love. I nicked it from the bottom of the pad. Careful—we don't want it looking dogeared, do we?'

Rose frowned and handed the certificate back. Antonia replaced it in her handbag and started the car.

'Aren't you going to say I'm a genius?'

Rose didn't answer.

'I mean, it couldn't be easier from now

on. We've cut out all the snags. We won't need a doctor's certificate. We fill in whatever we like and take it to the undertaker.'

'*What* couldn't be easier?'

Antonia smiled and swung the car into the traffic of Kensington High Street.

'Antonia, what couldn't be easier?'

'How would you like to meet my husband?'

11

ANTONIA was talking like a tour guide as she drove the Bentley up Portland Place and into Park Crescent. The route they were taking, she informed Rose, had been built by John Nash as a triumphal drive for that randy old swank the Prince Regent, all the way from St James's Park through Regent Street and Portland Place to what was planned to be a royal pleasure pavilion in Regent's Park. The Crescent had been conceived as a circus, but the funds ran out, so it was cut off halfway, and of course the pleasure pavilion was given the axe as well. Most of Nash's beautiful terraced houses had now been taken over by embassies, clubs and businesses.

Antonia's was one of the few still in use as a private home.

All this was lost on Rose. Her thinking had stopped at two death certificates, one with Barry's name on it, the other blank.

She'd been so preoccupied with what had happened in the past ten days that she'd failed entirely to see where it might lead. Barry's 'accident' had been a brilliant remedy for her troubles. Antonia had made it seem simple, doing what was necessary as if it were a common courtesy, like sharing an umbrella. Now, with the same serene indifference, Antonia was planning something else, and Rose was expected to join in. You can't share an umbrella without walking together.

The car door slammed. Antonia was already out and making an exaggerated gesture to Rose to follow.

'Come on. You need some strong coffee. You're looking more and more like that God-forsaken woman on the poster.'

'Well, the inquest was no picnic.'

Rose followed her between the twin columns at the entrance and up white steps into what could have passed as a set for one of those frothy films about the high life made to distract audiences from post-war austerity. She didn't believe real people lived in such opulence. You could have held a dance in the hall. The corniced ceiling was high enough to house two crystal chandeliers. There was a crimson carpet. Satin-striped wallpaper. An oval mahogany table with a silver tray for visiting cards.

Antonia tossed her fur coat over a chair. 'Hector insisted we furnish it in Regency. He's so hidebound. When we've got rid of him I'm going to strip it bare and start again. I want white walls and huge abstract paintings. Do you like Ben Nicholson?'

Rose missed the question. The skin at the back of her neck felt as if something had crawled across it.

'The painter, darling.'

Her legs started to shake. If she wasn't to make a complete idiot of herself she had to stay upright and mouth some words that would keep Antonia talking about the house. 'Who did you say?

'Ben Nicholson.'

'He's a painter, is he? I can't say I've heard of him.'

Antonia reached around Rose's shoulder and gently helped her off with her coat. 'Sweetie, you should never admit such ignorance. What you should say is, Nicholson's all right, but I prefer Stanley Spencer or Paul Nash or—who *do* you prefer?'

Rose's thoughts were still in turmoil. Name an artist. Any artist. She couldn't. 'I don't know anything about modern art.'

'Christ Almighty. Then you should definitely meet Hector. He thinks Picasso is something Italians eat. Make yourself at home in the sitting room—second door— and I'll see if he's in yet. He was supposed to be having lunch with a French professor. Ten to one he's sleeping it off.'

'Antonia, don't disturb him on my account. I'm sure there'll be another opportunity.'

There was a pause.

'The opportunity is now, my flower. It's got to be faced.'

She grasped Antonia's arm. 'Just a moment. I'd like to get this clear if you don't mind. What exactly has got to be faced?'

Antonia made light of it. 'Did I make him sound like an ogre? Don't worry—he's the one who should look out.'

Rose didn't pursue the question. Mentally she was reeling. She stepped into the room Antonia had indicated. It was as large as her own kitchen, sitting room and passage knocked into one. The dominant colours were blue and white. A tall clock startled her by chiming the quarter-hour. The date 1765 was painted on it in gold. Sets of china and silver were ranged about the walls in display cabinets. Waist-high Chinese vases that she took to be Ming stood on either side of the fireplace, where a white Persian cat was staring at the flames. It raised itself, arched, yawned and came to rub its head against her legs.

She stooped to run her fingers through the fur, wanting urgently to find some way of calming her nerves. She tried marshalling the few facts she'd learned about Hector: the meeting with Antonia on the steps of the air-raid shelter; his civilian status in the war; the death by drowning of his wife, whose name Rose had forgotten. To which could be added his ignorance of modern art and his lunch today with a French professor. And the evidence all around Rose that she had never been so close to real wealth.

Antonia pushed open the door. 'Just as I thought. He says he wants black coffee. How about you?'

'Coffee would be nice. Can I help?'

'No, I want to show off. We had a couple of servants until two weeks ago, a married couple, Irish. They took exception to something I said and walked out in a huff. Getting replacements is the very devil. However, I've learned how to make coffee, so I don't miss a chance to impress visitors. You can come and see the kitchen if you like.'

Rose stopped in the kitchen doorway and put her hands to her face. 'Oh, Antonia!'

'What's that? My fridge?'

It stood on stilts, a humming white cabinet of monumental size with a door like the front of a bank vault that Antonia needed two hands to unfasten and swing open. Rose gasped in awe at the intricate arrangement of shelves and trays inside, the Perspex storage boxes, the ice compartment and the place for bottles. For the moment her terrors were suspended.

'You like?'

She gave a start. Her nerves were in no state for surprises. Possibly the small man at her shoulder—who could be no one else but Hector—hadn't meant to startle her. He was so short that he'd slipped under her protective radar. She looked into a fleshy, smiling face framed in unruly reddish hair. Alert, brown intelligent eyes. Small, even teeth. A quite low-pitched voice with a strange intonation.

'You can order one from me. In production next year.'

Antonia slammed the fridge door. 'For Christ's sake, Hector, she lives in a matchbox. Rosie, this impetuous little man is my husband.'

Hector was unperturbed. Whether or not he understood, he treated her remark as a recommendation. 'Yes, I take orders now. Quality vacuum cleaners and fridges. Take the work out of housework. The only thing you hear from GEC, Prestcold, any of those companies is, fridges are on the way, worth waiting for, coming soon. Me, I take orders. How often do you wash your clothes? Soon I have a washing machine on the market better than anything in America. How do you do?'

They shook hands. He must have been ten years Antonia's senior, possibly more. Redheaded people carry their age well.

Rose was trying hard to place the accent. She hadn't expected a foreigner.

'I've never seen such an amazing fridge.'

'You like to see my high power vacuum cleaner?'

Antonia put a restraining hand on Hector's shoulder. In her heels she was cruelly taller than he. 'Hec, my cherub, you're boring my friend already. Why don't you take her into the sitting room and talk about something unmechanical while I brew up my delicious coffee?'

Out of earshot in the sitting room Rose confided to Hector that after all she would be interested to hear about his work.

'Are you sure?'

'Certain.'

'I thought so.' He pulled two chairs together and gestured to her to be seated. 'Antonia has heard it many times before. It's not news to her no more. You know, Rosie, engineering is in my blood. My father he had the first motor car in Prague. When I was still in short trousers he showed me how to strip. You understand?'

'Take the engine to pieces?'

'And assemble again. Clever boy, oily fingers, I went to technical school. Worked in a motor car factory seven years, made enough ackers to kiss my father goodbye, go to America. Detroit. Bloody hard work. Making automobiles by day, aeroplane parts by night. I worked six to midnight for a small guy starting up. Four, maybe five hours sleep, but no matter. This was one hell of a good time to be in aero-engineering. I had a brilliant idea for a carburettor nobody thought of.

So my friend says, Hec, why don't you give up making automobiles and be my partner? Half-share in the business. We shake hands and sign a paper. In two years, big profit. Big expansion. I expanded, too. Don't smile. I mean I got married. Maudie, a sweet girl from Detroit who wanted only one thing—to get the hell out of there. So I told my partner the problem. He bought me out and we sailed to England. 1931. *Mauretania.*'

'Romantic.'

Hector winked. 'Good business, too, Rosie. Plenty of customers for aero parts. I made the best carburettors Britain ever saw. I started a small factory in Surbiton, handy for Vickers. In seven years I had customers all over. I built factories in Birmingham, Southampton, Oxford. Many orders. Then the war came along. Aircraft production went crazy. Lord Beaverbrook cried out for carburettors. Everyone wanted carburettors. A. V. Roe, Vickers Supermarine, Handley Page, Fairey.'

Hector was warming to his story. The cat made a run for the door as Antonia came in with the coffee.

'Has he bored you stiff with his carburettors, darling? He talks about them the way other people talk about their operations.'

'I find it fascinating.'

'Liar. You don't have to stand on ceremony with us. Hec, do something useful and hand round the biscuits. I bet he hasn't said a word about your unhappy experience. You're all dressed up in black and he hasn't even asked why. You'd have to arrive in a hearse for him to take any interest and then he'd have the bonnet up to look at the carburettor. Hector, my friend Rose lost her husband last week, and when I say lost I mean he fell off the platform in the tube.'

'The tube. Oh, Jesus. Six hundred and thirty volts.'

'See the way his mind works?'

'It doesn't offend me.'

Rose smiled at Hector. To be fair, he'd looked distinctly concerned when he spoke of all those volts. If there was offence to be taken, it was at being invited to discuss his shortcomings in front of him as if he were deaf or stupid. He may have been socially out of step, but he had energy and honesty. She liked the disarming way he'd told his story, without the pretended modesty that most Englishmen seemed to feel was necessary when speaking about their

117

achievements. He'd earned his fortune through hard work and enterprise and wasn't ashamed to say so.

Now for some curious reason he was looking at Rose with awe.

He refused to be intimidated by Antonia. He found a way of excluding her just as blatantly as she'd talked over him. 'I feel close to you, Rosie. You and I, we both had the same experience.'

Antonia thrust a cup of coffee towards Rose. 'He means his wife had an accident, too. Careful how you drink this stuff. It's out of a bottle. I won't blame you if you spit it out.'

She took a sip. 'It's not at all bad.'

Hector held out the biscuits. 'These help to disguise the taste. She drowned, my Maudie.'

'How dreadful.' In common decency she felt obliged to react as if she hadn't heard the information before. She just hoped Antonia wouldn't take her up on it.

'It was in a swimming pool. In the war I had this country house in Hampshire for weekends. Nice grounds. Nice pool. Long way from Portsmouth and Southampton. Pretty safe from bombing. Our friends came sometimes. Maudie liked to give parties.' He glanced across at Antonia, which was a mistake because she slickly took over the story.

'She'd had a skinful, and that's no exaggeration, darling. She'd been on rum and peppermint, of all things. She couldn't have swum a stroke if she'd tried.'

'Did anyone see what happened?'

'Most of us were on the terrace dancing to the gramophone. One of the staff spotted her lying on the bottom soon after midnight. Six feet down.'

'Six feet six.'

'There speaks the engineer again. Hector, dear, you shouldn't say things like that. It gives an appalling impression, as if you didn't care. Of course we both know that couldn't be further from the truth. It wasn't his fault she was so depressed.'

Hector gave a nod. 'Time to change the subject, eh? Rosie, do you like to cook?'

'Well, when I could get eggs and things, yes.'

'We can get plenty. Butter. Sugar.'

Antonia sighed. 'There you go again.'

'What's wrong now?'

'Rosie's going to think we're on the black market, that's what's wrong. The fact is, Rose, that I'm the world's worst cook, so we generally go to restaurants. I never get through my ration books.'

Hector grinned. 'Biggest fridge in London. Bugger all in it.'

He got a glare from Antonia.

Rose laughed. Why take offence? She and Antonia had heard plenty worse in the old days. She was suddenly aware how much those few minutes with Hector had relaxed her. She'd been terribly strung-up before.

She smiled happily. 'I don't blame you. I'd bloody well eat out as well if I could afford it.'

'Why don't you come out with us, then?' Antonia suggested.

'Oh, I didn't mean that.'

'Don't be so coy. We'd like your company, wouldn't we, Hec?'

'But of course! Tomorrow?' His sharp eyes shone at the prospect.

She was ambushed by their solidarity. 'I couldn't possibly before the funeral. Perhaps later in the week?'

'Saturday.'

Soon after this was agreed, Hector had to answer the phone. Antonia got up.

'You look all in, darling. I'll drive you back to Pimlico.'

In the Bentley, Rose tried to launch a bland, undemanding conversation.

'I love your house.'

'Who wouldn't?' Antonia didn't pause. She came straight out with it. 'What do you think of my husband?'

The tension clamped Rose again like pincers. What was she expected to say? 'I didn't realize you'd married a foreigner. He's so different from most Englishmen.'

'God, I hope so!'

'He made me welcome.'

'He would, so long as you listen to his tedious life story and coo at intervals. I'm sick of it. It drives me up the wall. That and his vacuum cleaners.'

'Do you think he knows?'

'Of course he does. He's so full of himself that he doesn't give a shit.'

'I'm sorry.'

'Sweetie, I'm not fishing for sympathy. I didn't waste any on you, did I?'

Rose looked away, not wanting to go into what Antonia had done in lieu of sympathy. 'Doesn't it get dark early now? It's not even five o'clock.'

'I want an end to it.'

'A divorce?'

'No chance of that. It's against his religion. He's a Catholic. Doesn't go to church or eat fish on Fridays, but when it comes to divorce, he's unshakeable. It's against God's law. That's how he was brought up.'

'Have you asked him? If it doesn't mean so much to him now, perhaps he'd see his way to giving you a divorce.'

'What use is that to me? I'd lose everything and have to pay the costs.'

'Why?'

'I'd be the guilty party, wouldn't I?'

'You mean . . . ?'

'You know what I mean. Let's face it, Rose. I've got a lover. To put it in legal claptrap I've committed adultery on a number of occasions. No prizes for guessing the name of the fascinating man.'

'Does Hector know?'

'He turns a blind eye. The only way it would come to his attention is if he found us at it in his precious fridge, or doing something naughty with the vacuum cleaner.'

'There may be other grounds. Has he ever been cruel to you?'

'Hector?' She found this amusing.

Now Rose had started, she felt obliged to continue. 'Is there any chance that he's been with someone else? There must be plenty of designing women who'd fancy a man with his money.' She wished immediately that she'd kept her mouth shut.

'Like I did, you mean?' Antonia let the question hang in the air just long enough to give Rose a wrench of embarrassment, then dismissed it. 'No, darling, no vultures circling overhead. I'd know.'

Mercifully the conversation stopped for the traffic at Piccadilly Circus. When they'd crossed to the Haymarket, Rose changed to a different tack.

'I'd be glad if you'd put me down in Victoria Street. I'd like to get these documents to the undertaker.'

'Whatever you want, my dear.'

'Thanks.'

Antonia added, 'By the way, I shan't be coming to Barry's funeral.'

'That's all right. I didn't expect you.'

'It doesn't mean I've lost interest.'

'I know.'

'And no disrespect meant to Barry.' She slowed for a traffic light. 'It's a burial, I take it?'

'Yes. Just a few people.'

'Brompton Cemetery?'

'Yes.'

'Poor old Barry. Grounded at last.' The

light changed to green. 'I'm going to have Hector cremated.'

12

On the night before the funeral Rose was surprised to get a phone call from Rex Ballard, one of the Kettlesham Heath pilots, a Squadron Leader who it turned out was still serving there. He had heard about Barry's death from his sister who worked in the coroner's office. He remembered Rose, of course. He said he would be driving up from Suffolk in the morning with three old chums from Battle of Britain days. Rose tried explaining that it was to be a quiet family funeral. Rex was not to be put off. In that case, he said, there would be room at the graveside for a few old friends who wanted to pay their respects, wouldn't there?

The 'old friends' had grown to fourteen by the time they gathered around the grave in Brompton Cemetery. Three civil service people from the Stationery Office who Rose had never seen before stood rigidly at one end with their furled umbrellas in front of them like reversed rifles. The Irish couple who lived two doors away in Oldfield Gardens and never missed a thing had turned up, thoughtfully with only two of their six children. Also, wearing black armbands, one of the barmen and two regulars from The Orange, where Barry used to drink. Then the quartet from the RAF, stouter and redder in the face than they'd looked in 1940 and now without a moustache between them.

The family group consisted of Barry's stepsister Daphne and her obnoxious husband Ronald, Rose's parents and Aunt Joan. And Rose herself.

Her father had offered to read the service. She'd said at the risk of hurting him that she would find the whole thing too distressing. She preferred to have the words spoken by a priest she didn't know. Daddy nodded and said he understood. Rose hoped to God that he didn't and never would.

Even then it was an ordeal going through the motions of lament with them beside her and everyone watching for evidence of grief from the wretched widow. She kept her head bowed and bit her lip and dabbed her face with a hankie. They were genuine tears. The ritual hardly touched her, but she wept for all the lies she would be forced to tell before the afternoon was out.

They all said afterwards how splendidly brave she had been.

Her mother and aunt had helped her prepare some food at the house for after the funeral. Spam sandwiches mostly, plates of digestive biscuits and slabs of trench cake. The cake was her mother's contribution, from a First World War recipe that the Ministry of Food had disinterred for the Second. It was made without eggs and Mother rashly announced that the original trench cakes had kept for three months on the Western Front. No one enquired why they hadn't been eaten in all that time, but when she offered to pass the recipe on there was an embarrassing silence. Only the Irish children tried any.

Much against her desire, Rose remained the centre of attention. Offers of support were showered on her.

'I want you to know, my dear, that we at the Stationery Office wouldn't want you to get into difficulties. If there's anything that needs attention, my name is Gascoigne and this is McGill and our young colleague here is Tremlett. Remember, won't you? Anything under the sun.'

She had an engaging picture of Gascoigne, McGill and Tremlett under the sun, bare-chested on the roof replacing the war-damaged tiles.

'So kind.'

'Not at all. Barry was held in the highest esteem at the depot. We shall not look upon his like again, as the Bard expressed it. Now that we know each other. . . .'

The bonhomie was excessive, like Victory Day all over again. Why am I so cynical? Rose asked the kettle as she filled it.

As for the RAF mourners, they had their own way of combating depression. They took turns going out to the car to top up with something from a bottle. Out of re-spect for the cloth, as they put it (meaning Daddy, who could see very well what was going on, and wouldn't have been averse to a nip), they used teacups and let it be known that they were drinking Russian tea.

'Never would have guessed your Pop was a parson, Rose. You should have told us, you know.'

'Why?'

'Freddie here would have moderated his language.'

'Did he say something? I didn't hear him.'

'Lord, no. He's been the soul of discretion today. I'm talking about the war. In the ops room. The things you heard must have made your toes curl.'

Rose shook her head. 'Let's make no bones about it, we were all living on our nerves. I said a few strong words myself when I was pressed.'

'My dear, I never heard them pass your lips. But you're right about the pressures. Say what you like about our flying skills, we needed the luck of Old Nick to survive. Dear old Barry, rest his soul, was in the thick of it and came through triumphant every blessed time. Even when he got in trouble he limped back somehow, hours late, with that beautiful fatuous grin on his face. He was indestructible.'

'So were you, as it turned out.'

'Yes, but we could all name plenty of good lads who didn't make it home. If there's any sense in it all, we're bound to ask why we were spared.'

'Rex, I'd better get round with the tea before it gets cold.'

'Just a moment, dear. I'm shockingly hamfisted with words, I know. Always was. What I'm getting at is this. Somehow we *knew* Barry would always come back. He gave you that sense of living a charmed life. So when I was told he'd fallen off a railway platform, I couldn't believe my ears. The Piccadilly Line? Dear old Barry? That's not like him, I said, not like him at all.'

'Accidents happen all the time.'

'Not to the likes of Barry. To tell the truth, I still haven't taken it in properly. Standing there in the cemetery this afternoon I kept thinking, this isn't right. Any minute I'm going to feel a tap on my shoulder and I'll turn round and it'll be old Barry in his flying kit having a bloody good laugh at us.'

One of the others, Peter Bliss, had been getting restless. 'Put a sock in it, Rex.'

'What's up?'

'You're talking baloney.'

'Pardon me, old son, but it's a fact. Barry always came back. Always.'

'This is hardly the time and place to go on about it.'

Rose gave Bliss a nod of thanks and moved off to fill the teapot again. She found her mother in the kitchen washing plates with Aunt Joan. An opportunity, Mummy had decided, for a heart-to-heart.

'Now that it's over, we want you to come home with us for at least a few weeks, my pet. You look so dreadful, I can hardly believe it's my own daughter.'

'Mummy, I appreciate the thought.'

'It's more than a thought, dear. I absolutely insist, and so does your father.'

'I know you mean well, but it's out of the question. There's too much to be done here.'

'Nothing that can't wait. I couldn't possibly go away tonight and leave you alone in this dreadful . . . I mean, in this house with . . . with so many memories.'

Aunt Joan came tactfully to her sister's aid. 'It was that face on the hoarding across the road that upset us. So depressing for you to look out on all the time.'

'The widow? I've got used to her now. She doesn't bother me in the least. Really.'

'As if we haven't all seen enough horrors since the war ended.'

'I'll manage perfectly well by myself, Mummy.'

'It isn't as if you have friends you can turn to. I don't mind telling you I don't take to those Irish people.'

'They're neighbours. I'm not without friends, believe me.

'Friends? Up here in London? Who, for instance?'

'Um, people you wouldn't know. Ex-service.'

She was too late to bite back the last words.

Her mother gave her a sharp look. God, how much longer would the kettle take? She tried turning the gas up. It was already fully on.

The cross-questioning began in earnest. 'Air Force people then?'

'Yes.'

'Ex-service, you said. You don't mean the men in the other room?'

'No.'

'WAAFs?'

'You wouldn't know them, Mummy.'

'I didn't see any WAAFs here today.'

'They couldn't manage it. Would you be a dear and put out some more biscuits? We're about to run out in the other room.'

'There's plenty of cake left. They've hardly touched it. Do you really want to use up all the biscuits? All right, if that's what you want. We'll talk about this again, dear. I'm far from satisfied.'

Rose filled the teapot and went in search of the civil servants. They'd managed to corner her father and were telling him about the inner workings of the Stationery Office. He was reacting with every muscle of his face, as if no subject interested him more passionately. By the nature of his occupation he was a splendid listener. She'd watched him earlier doing his stuff with the Air Force. Dear, generous-hearted Daddy.

It would be folly to go home with her parents, sweet as they were. Between Mummy's sharp questions and Daddy's spirituality she'd be confessing everything before the train left Waterloo.

What a shock they'd get! She had never so much as hinted that the marriage was unhappy. The few Saturday afternoons she'd taken Barry back to the Rectory he'd played the part of the loving husband and she'd been grateful for the effort he put into it. The fact that he'd spent the previous evening in the arms of a tart in some hotel room seemed as unthinkable as Daddy dropping an 'h' or Mummy a stitch.

How, then, could they even begin to comprehend the truth about Barry's death and her part in it?

Gascoigne the civil servant appeared beside her. 'My colleagues and I will be leaving in a few minutes, Mrs Bell.'

'Thank you for coming.'

'It was a pleasure.' He coughed. 'That is to say, thank you for your hospitality. One small matter I wished to mention. Mr Bell left a few personal items in his desk including a photograph that may be of some sentimental value, a fountain pen and, I think, some tickets for a dance. I placed them in an envelope for safe keeping.'

'I don't suppose they're important.'

'Ah, but I wouldn't want to dispose of them without your seeing them.'

'Could you put them in the post?'

'I'm concerned about the possibility of the pen leaking over the other things. Would you like me to arrange for someone from the depot to bring them here? It didn't seem appropriate today.'

'That's all right. I'll come to the depot and see if they're worth keeping.'

'Really? I don't want to put you to any trouble.'

'I'll let you know when I'm coming.'

After repeating his offer to do anything of practical help that Rose could think of, Gascoigne gathered McGill and Tremlett and left. For a moment it appeared as if the Kettlesham Heath crowd were lining up to say goodbye as well. Not so. Rex Ballard still had something on his mind.

'I suppose you haven't run into any of the girls lately?'

'The girls?'

'WAAFs, my dear. Your fellow-plotters.'

Rose's pulse beat faster. Rex was one of

those people who put you at ease and then poleaxed you with something he'd discovered. He'd found out about the funeral. What else did he know?

'I think we all went our own ways. One met so many people in the war.'

'True.' He looked wistful. 'They're a very insipid bunch on the station now. No sense of fun. I wouldn't mind having a get-together one weekend with some of the war-time crowd. A sort of reunion. Do you think it's a good idea?'

Was that all he meant? The relief!

'I'd need to think about it.'

'We'd have to find out where they are now, of course. You've lost touch with everyone, have you?'

With uncanny timing, her mother pushed a plate of trench cake between them. 'Far from it, Squadron Leader. Rose was telling me just now that her ex-service friends are all she's got in London, weren't you, dear?'

Rose sidestepped. 'Mummy, we're talking about Kettlesham Heath now, not Hornchurch. I met Rex at Kettlesham Heath.'

'Oh, I'm out of order as usual, am I? Have some cake anyway.'

'It looks delicious. Unfortunately I'm not

the cake-eating type, Mrs Mason, but I say, if there's another spam sandwich . . .'

While her mother went off to cut more bread, Rose let it be understood that a squadron reunion wasn't to her liking. She told Rex candidly that she'd regard it as an ordeal rather than a pleasure. He said he sympathized. However, in case she changed her mind later, he'd let her know if the idea came to anything. Soon after, the RAF party set off for Suffolk in their Standard 12.

When her parents finally left with Aunt Joan they all but dragged her off the door-step and into their small car. She escaped by undertaking to visit them at the earliest opportunity. They also extracted promises that she would say her prayers each night and finish every crumb of the trench cake. She thought, I'll need more than prayers if I do.

13

ALONE in the sitting room Rose threw off her shoes and collapsed on the settee. Her legs ached, her head was ringing from being the focus of so much conversation, but the sensation of relief was like champagne. Barry was buried and the funeral was over.

She was beginning to think that she'd reward herself with a sherry before facing the washing-up when she heard a sound from upstairs. Someone was in her bedroom. What she'd heard was the loose floorboard in front of the wardrobe.

It frightened her. She'd quite convinced herself she was alone in the house. She sat up, reached for her shoes and put them on, at the same time checking mentally which of the guests had definitely left. She glanced out of the window. No cars were left in the street.

Another creak from the floorboard.

She couldn't fathom who it could be, or why they should be where they were. The noise definitely hadn't come from the bathroom. Whoever was up there was creeping about, not wanting to be discovered.

That stupid remark of Rex Ballard's crept into her mind, about Barry always coming back. Stupid and irresponsible. This time Barry couldn't possibly come back.

Yet she'd heard that board creak a thousand times before and it had always been Barry upstairs.

She stood with her hand on the banister rail, listening. She ought to have called out and asked who was there. Her throat wouldn't function. She was going to have to go upstairs and look inside that bedroom. If she didn't face it now, she'd never be able to sleep in the house again.

The landing light was on, but that meant nothing. It had got dark in the last hour. people would have needed the light to use the bathroom.

She told herself this had to be done. Without pausing, she mounted the stairs, crossed the landing and opened the bedroom door.

The light wasn't on in there. The light from the landing picked out the figure of a man in front of the wardrobe dressed in Barry's demob jacket.

Rose caught her breath and took a step back.

'What are you doing?'

He turned. 'Hello, Rose.'

It wasn't Barry, of course. It was Barry's oafish brother-in-law, Ronald. And Daphne, his harpy of a wife, stepped out of the shadows and took her place beside him. They'd been in there in the dark, communicating in whispers.

'Has everyone gone, then?'

'I supposed they had.'

137

'Didn't you know we were still here?'

'Hope we didn't frighten you, Rose.'

'What the hell are you doing in my bedroom?'

Ronald was a master of the art of bluffing his way out of embarrassing situations. He had plenty of practice, for his manners had always been abysmal. 'Merely trying on one or two of Barry's jackets, my dear. Seeing that you'll have no further use for them, I thought I'd offer to make some room in the wardrobe. It's not a bad fit really, is it?'

'Take it off.'

'There's no need to take offence, Rose.'

'Isn't there? Who invited you up here? I didn't.'

Daphne, long resentful of Rose annexing her brother, bared her claws. 'We didn't expect you would. Barry wouldn't have thought twice about it. He was sweet-natured.'

'Get out of my house, both of you.'

'*Your* house now, is it? That tripped off the tongue very easily. How do you know it's yours? Have you seen the will?'

'There isn't a will.'

'No will? I find that hard to believe.'

'Frankly, Daphne, I don't care what you believe.'

'I suppose you think you'll inherit every-thing. Well, you've made a serious mistake. As his only blood relative, I shall instruct my solicitor to begin proceedings. I'm enti-tled to my share and I intend to claim it.'

'Your share of what—his debts?'

Daphne gave a cry like a seagull. 'My brother wasn't in debt.'

'He was overdrawn several hundred pounds. If I were you I should think twice before you go to the expense of a solicitor.'

Ronald peeled off Barry's jacket, held it at arm's length as if it were flearidden and let it drop in a heap on the bed. He picked up his own and took Daphne by the arm. 'Better leave it for the present, old girl.'

Daphne ignored the advice. 'Barry couldn't possibly be in debt. He was an ex-officer, for God's sake. A civil servant. None of this rings true, Ronald. She's lying. He must have left a will. All those pilots who risked their lives in the war left wills. I believe she's destroyed it, that's what she's done.'

'Steady, Daph.'

'I'm going to get to the bottom of this.'

Rose was unmoved. 'At this minute, Daphne, you're going to get to the bottom of the stairs and straight out of my house.'

'With the utmost pleasure. I don't wish to remain in it a minute longer.'

Watching from the front room window as they retreated up Oldfield Gardens to catch a bus, Rose doubted if she would hear from either of them again. She returned to the kitchen and took out the sherry. On second thoughts, she put it back. She'd already given herself the boost she needed.

Sleep was slow in coming. Fragments of conversation flitted in and out of her brain. At about two in the morning she got up and made some tea. She carried it into the front room and got out the writing pad. She was in no way depressed. She felt strong. She'd been firm with her parents. And in giving Daphne and Ronald their marching orders she'd discovered something new in her personality. Now she was ready to take up the pen.

27 Oldfield Gardens,
Pimlico,
London SW1.
Dear Miss Paxton,

Although we haven't met, Barry told me about you and your child. I am his lawful wife—or was. I am sorry to inform

140

you that Barry was killed in an accident in the underground on Thursday, 16th October. The funeral took place yesterday at Brompton Cemetery. I understand what a shock this must be for you.

Barry made no will. Even if he had, the state of his bank account would have rendered it meaningless, for he was overdrawn seven hundred pounds.

Believe me when I say I am in no position to assist you or the boy. I can only repeat in sincerity that I am sorry.

Yours truly,
Rose Bell

It didn't take long to write. When she had finished, she soon fell asleep on the settee.

14

SHORTLY before 7.30 on Tuesday morning a taxi entered Hyde Park by the Cumberland Gate, drove around the Ring and halted just across the bridge over the Serpentine. Antonia, who was the passenger, sensibly remained inside wrapped in her mink, for there was a thick frost. Her breath was making ice on the window. She rubbed at it.

'A little closer, driver.'

'You wouldn't be thinking of joining them, miss?'

'No fear.'

The all-weather bathers were taking their dip. A dozen at least, including women, were in the water paddling joylessly about.

The driver stopped at the point closest to the water. 'Like ruddy lobsters, except that this lot go in red and come out blue.'

Some minutes passed. It seemed to be a case of first out's a cissy. Then two of the women waded to the bank and started the exodus.

Antonia sighed. 'They get no credit for this unless they break the ice to go in. Then they get their picture in the papers.'

'I can think of easier ways, miss.'

One of the last to emerge was Vic, wearing trunks and chatting to two middle-aged men in old-fashioned costumes with shoulder straps. Although Antonia inclined to the view that people who did this must be cold-blooded or mad, or both, she wasn't totally disapproving. Vic's body was good to look at even in these conditions. There was a suggestion of power as he moved, and his damp body-hair darkened the flesh and picked out the muscles as he flexed them.

She wound down the window and called his name.

He stopped and stared. Then he recognized her and gestured that he needed to dry himself. She nodded. He went into the brick bathing house to change.

The driver had watched all this with interest. 'Boyfriend, miss!

'Sort of.'

'Funny time to meet.'

'I spent most of yesterday trying to find him.' She took out her cigarettes and offered him one. 'He'd better not be long.'

'Doing up his buttons won't be easy with frozen fingers.'

'Don't worry. He'll get a roasting from me.'

She stared across the steely sheet of water until Vic emerged from the bathing house in his overcoat and came over to the taxi and climbed in.

'Well, this is an unexpected pleasure. What are you doing here?' He leaned across to kiss her cheek.

She withdrew her face out of range. 'Making one final attempt to track you down.'

'You were looking for me?'

'For the last twenty-four hours.'

'Sorry. I was sent to Birmingham. A conference. I got back at eleven last night.'

'You could have picked up a phone.'

The voice from the front interjected, 'Where to, please?'

She clicked her tongue impatiently. 'I suppose you're ravenous for breakfast now.'

The driver switched on his engine. 'There's a place at the top of North End Road. It ain't the Savoy, but you'll never taste a better bacon and egg.'

Later, after they'd put this recommendation to the test, Antonia conceded that the driver hadn't been far wrong. Her pleasure in the meal was much assisted by a full apology from Vic.

She forgave him, and more. 'I'm coming to stay with you some time in the next week or so.'

'To *stay?*'

'Yes, won't it be divine? Our first whole night together. Then our second and our third and—'

'What's Hector going to say about this?'

'I haven't spoken to him yet. He won't be any trouble.'

Vic glanced around the small café. Some traders from the market in wide-boy overcoats with heavily padded shoulders were in for breakfast. No one seemed to be listening.

'Antonia, I'd like to know more about this. Are you up to something?'

'Of course I'm up to something. I want to marry you and go to America.'

'Yes, but I don't want some bastard with a flash-camera bursting into my flat and taking pictures of you and me in bed.'

She laughed. 'How did you get that dopey idea?'

'That's the way people arrange it these days.'

'Arrange what?'

'Divorce.'

'Sweetie, how many times do I have to tell you divorce is out of the question? Forget about men with cameras.'

He sighed. 'I don't understand it.'

She lodged her foot against his. 'Don't try. Simply enjoy it while you've got the chance.'

Mr Smart, the insurance agent, was on the doorstep again, in the act of raising his trilby as Rose opened the door. His nose and ears were pillarbox red.

'Good day, Mrs Bell. Bright but cold. Ice about.'

'You'd better come in.'

He placed his hat and bicycle pump on the hallstand and removed his clips. 'How are you settling down?'

'I'm managing the best I can. Would you care for a cup of tea?'

'That sounds agreeable.'

'If you don't mind the kitchen, it's warmer in there.'

He stood rubbing his hands by the boiler. The teacloths from yesterday's wash-up were draped from the struts attached to the flue.

Rose reached for the matches and lit the gas under the kettle. 'What have you got— more forms for me to fill in?'

'I require no more than a signature this time. The funeral was yesterday, I believe.'

'Yes.'

'I dare say you're glad it's over.'

She detected an undercurrent of disapproval in the voice.

'It kept me busy. I was grateful for that.'

'Stopped your mind from dwelling on things.'

'True.'

'Are you able to get any sleep at all?'

She gave him a long, cool look. 'While we're waiting for the kettle, Mr Smart, don't you think we should get down to business?'

'As you wish. This is what you are waiting for, I think.' He took a brown envelope from his pocket and placed it ostentatiously on the kitchen table. 'Your cheque for five thousand pounds.'

She resisted the polite impulse to say thank you. Why should she? Nor did she snatch up the envelope and rip it open. She put out cups and saucers and went to the larder for milk.

'I shall require your signature on the receipt.'

'Naturally.' She noticed her Coronation biscuit tin taking up room at the front of the larder and remembered what it contained. 'A piece of cake?'

Mr Smart unexpectedly laughed, and there wasn't any humour in the laugh. 'Tell me, is that an offer of something to eat—or self-congratulation?'

She felt the blood drain from her face. 'What exactly do you mean?'

He gave a superior smile. 'A piece of cake. One of those cheerful phrases the RAF has given the language. Is that what all this has been, Mrs Bell? A piece of cake?'

She clenched her teeth. She thought, I've been through a police interrogation, an inquest and a funeral. Am I to be tripped by this pipsqueak insurance man? He's only guessing. He can't be certain. She prised the lid off the tin and held her mother's trench cake in front of him.

He selected a slice. There was a sneer on his face, as if the act of handing over the cheque had absolved him of the need to curry favour. 'Strictly between ourselves, I've come across some queer things in the insurance business, but this is one of the queerest. The very day your husband is due to surrender his policy, he's killed in an accident. Astonishing. You can hardly blame my company for wanting to make sure of the facts. We put the case in the hands of our best investigators. They find that the only person who stands to benefit—no sugar, if that's my cup—has a watertight alibi. Sorry, I shouldn't use the word "alibi". It implies that an offence was committed and we know it wasn't, don't we? The coroner was satisfied, his jury were satisfied and our investigators were unable to prove that anything irregular had happened.'

So it was supposition. He knew nothing about Antonia.

'Then I suggest, Mr Smart, that you stop imagining things.' Rose pushed the tea towards him. She reached for her handbag and took out her fountain pen. 'Do you have that receipt?'

'In the envelope.'

He finished his tea and left without touching the cake.

Some time after midnight Hector stopped work in his office downstairs and came to bed. He undressed in the dark, padding about in his shirt-tails so as not to disturb Antonia.

He didn't disturb her because she was still awake. She lay in silence in her own bed with her eyes open, waiting. The plan of action she was shortly to outline to Hector required his total concentration. She wanted him passive, in bed, where he had no choice except to listen. He had to be made to understand that his part in the plan was not only necessary, but inescapable.

She waited two or three minutes after he'd climbed into bed.

'Hec.'

'Mm?'

'What did you think of Rose?'

'Who?'

'My pretty little friend from the WAAF.'

'Rosie Bell? Nice girl. Why ask me?'

'I've decided to kill her.'

149

The bedsprings screeched. 'You gone mad?'

'I knew you'd say that. Listen, will you? It's the perfect answer to our problem. We invite her here to cook for you while I'm away.'

'You're going to *kill* her?'

'Pipe down and listen. I said I'm going away for a few days.'

'Going away? Where?'

'I'll come to that. I won't really be away. Not far, anyway. I've arranged to stay somewhere near. We give Rose the key and she lets herself in to make you a pie or something. I saw the way she looked at you when you asked if she could cook. She'll do it for you. I'll be hiding in the house. I surprise her and knock her out with chloroform. Then I smother her with a cushion. No blood. No mess.'

'Antonia, this is raving mad, you know.'

'No, it isn't, and I'll tell you why. I've managed to get hold of a blank death certificate.'

'A doctor's certificate?'

'No. Get a grip on yourself, Hector, and *listen*. A death registration. The one the registry office issues. With that we can get a body buried. We fill it in ourselves. We

150

won't even need a doctor's certificate. It's quite straightforward.'

'You think?'

'I'm certain.'

'But it's wicked to think of killing that poor sweet girl. What has Rosie done to hurt you or me? Nothing. She trusts us.'

'Poor, sweet girl! Hector, you're a mutt. That sweet girl is bloody dangerous. She's got to be stopped.'

'Stopped? What is she doing?'

'Any day now she'll go to the police.' Antonia took a deep breath. 'My fault, I admit it. I was taken in like you. Stupidly I let something slip about Maudie's death.'

Hector groaned. 'Maudie! Oh, no! You opened your big mouth. Crazy!'

Smoothly and expertly, Antonia embroidered fiction over the facts. 'Days ago I made some remark about having to wait for Maudie to die before you and I could marry. Then of course she met you and almost the first thing you told her was that Maudie drowned. I don't blame you, Hec, but she was on to it at once. She won't let it pass. She's been pestering me about it ever since. She's that sort of person. I'm certain she knows already.'

'Would she really go to the police?'

151

'You've met her. She's a vicar's daughter. A model bloody citizen. She'd regard it as her moral duty. She's got to be stopped, Hec.'

His reply was muffled, as if he'd pressed his hands to his face. 'I can't do this, Antonia.'

'You don't have to. I'm doing it. It's too bloody late to discover you have a conscience.'

He was silent for a long time.

'All right, you crazy bitch. After you kill Rosie in this house, what do you say to her people? She tripped over the cat and fell downstairs? She choked on a fish bone? You think her mother and father are going to believe you? And who arranges the funeral? You can't take this certificate to the undertaker and get her buried yourself.'

'No, my sweet. That's your job.'

'*Mine?* You make a big mistake there.'

'Calm down and listen to me, little man. You've jumped to all the wrong conclusions. Give me credit for some intelligence. There will be no trouble from Rosie's people because they won't know she's dead. The name on the death certificate will be mine. It will be *my* funeral, Hector. Can you get that into your head?'

He took a huge breath and then exhaled in a series of nervous bursts.

Antonia was in no hurry to move on. She wanted the essential message to sink in first. He was not unintelligent.

When he spoke again his tone was sceptical, but he'd got the point. 'Her body, your funeral.'

'Exactly. That's why you must make the arrangements. It isn't much to do, considering what you get in return. No more worries over the Maudie business. And you'll be a single man again. A widower for the second time. We were talking about it only the other day. A life of your own, you old goat. You'll never hear from me again.'

'Oh yes? Where will you go?'

'America, with Vic.'

'They won't let you stay.'

'Don't fret over that. I'll be married to him and he's got that job at Princeton.'

'Married?'

'Birdbrain. Haven't you worked it out? I'll be using Rose's identity. It's simply a matter of going through her handbag after she's dead. Her identity card will be there. If by any chance it isn't, the key of her house is sure to be, and I'll collect it the same evening and become sweet little Rosie Bell.

153

I'll marry Vic at a registry office somewhere outside London within a couple of days. New surname. New passport. New country. Isn't it neat?'

'What about her people? They will report that she's missing.'

'Hector, thousands of people are missing. Haven't you ever looked at those lists in the Sunday papers? The police can't keep up with it. What's one more missing woman?'

He gave up trying to pick fault with the plan. He turned obstinate instead. 'I won't do this, Antonia. It's a mortal sin. I should never have let you kill poor Maudie. I suffer terrible dreams for that. I can't stand by and let you repeat that wicked thing.'

'Come off it, Hector! Don't get high and mighty with me now. It doesn't wash. We're in this together.'

'Not together. Leave me out.'

'How can I? Be reasonable. I can't arrange my own funeral.'

There was another scrunch from the bedsprings as he kicked out in fury. 'You tell *me* be reasonable? Killing another innocent woman—is that reasonable?'

'She's not so innocent as you think, but that's not the point. I'm going to insist that you help me in this, Hector. You and I are going to make it happen exactly as I told you. I shall definitely kill her. If anything goes wrong, if you fail me, I swear to God I'll see you swing for killing Maudie.'

'Maudie! *You* pushed her in the pool!'

'With your connivance. You wanted to get rid of her. You were sick of her black moods and her drinking. I told you what I was going to do. That made you an accessory before the fact of murder, Hector. That's a hanging offence.'

'I didn't know how serious you were.'

'You stood back and let me get on with it. An English court of law isn't going to waste much sympathy on a nasty little foreigner who gets his mistress to do the dirty work for him. I might get away with a life sentence, but it's the rope for you, make no mistake about that.'

She let him brood on that. When he spoke again it was with an air of resignation.

'Say what you want. Exactly.'

She went over her plan minutely. And after she'd told him the undemanding but necessary part she wanted him to play, she added that she also required twenty thousand pounds to get settled in America.

He was silent.

She said it would be a once and for all

payment. He would never hear from her again.

He said she could have it. Then he called her a bloodsucking monster.

She wished him a cheery goodnight.

15

ROSE'S nerves had given her another bad night. On Wednesday morning she needed to do something to occupy her mind so she went to Gorringe's and blued two clothing coupons and some of her new wealth on a roll of parachute silk. She'd decided to run up a set of underclothes on the sewing machine. Her dreary Utility things would go into service as floorcloths. Walking around the shop she drew up a mental shopping list, a wardrobe for the good times ahead. After a decent interval she would get a 'long look' coat, a suit with padded hips and shoulders, a couple of day dresses in bright prints and some shiny sling-back shoes. But the silk undies came first. It would create a bad impression to break out too soon after burying Barry. She didn't want the likes of Mr Sharp spreading rumours. Yet she couldn't wait to blot out every memory of Barry, throw out all the clothes she'd worn while she was married to him and start afresh. Well, some silk undies would be a start. No one need know what she was wearing underneath. Not without an invitation, she told herself in an effort to be frivolous. People were always telling her she was too solemn. She went straight up to Haberdashery and bought five yards of lace trimming.

She snipped and machined all afternoon with the firm intention of wearing her handiwork on Saturday when Antonia and Hector took her out to dinner. Up to now she'd been intimidated by Antonia's clothes. It would be a confidence boost to wear silk under her dreary old suit.

She was going to have no nonsense from Antonia, she decided. A week's respite from that domineering presence had given her a chance to think for herself. Antonia was clearly playing some elaborate and tasteless charade. She had always enjoyed shocking others, but that remark about having Hector cremated had been the limit. And that dangerous escapade to obtain the blank death registration certificate was obviously part of the same ghoulish game.

Wasn't it?

It was horrid to talk about doing away

with Hector as if he were just as expendable as Barry. The two couldn't be compared. Barry had degenerated dangerously. He'd started to get violent. There would have been no escape. But Hector offered no threat whatsoever. He'd done nothing despicable that Rose had heard of. In fact he appeared rather charming. His worst fault, it seemed, was that he talked too much about his work —hardly a capital crime. Antonia was bored with him. She wanted to be rid of him, but there was a catch. She also wanted his money, to keep on living like a countess. Not a nice reason for killing anyone.

That, in Rose's eyes, would be a very wicked murder. Of course it was nonsense. It had to be.

She had an unpleasant shock on Friday. The doorbell rang at lunchtime and when she answered it she saw two children with the lifeless body of an adult man between them. They were trying with difficulty to support him at the armpits. His head hung over his chest and his knees had buckled under him. He was dressed in a grey trilby, shirt, trousers and boots. The elder child grabbed the head and jerked it upright.

'Penny for the Guy, miss.'

The face was a crudely drawn mask. The body was stuffed.

'Bonfire Night.'

'Isn't it rather early for that? It's still October.'

They were the Irish children from two doors along. They stood staring at her.

'I'll see what I've got in my purse. Did you make him yourselves?'

'Yes, miss.'

'He doesn't look very warm, dressed like that, in just a shirt. Wait a minute. I've got an idea.'

She returned presently with Barry's demob jacket, the garment Ronald had been caught in the act of trying on. 'See if this fits.'

'That's too good for the Guy, miss.'

'I've no use for it. Look, it suits him.' She laughed. 'And here's a tie. He'll look smart in a tie.'

In Barry's jacket and RAF tie, he looked distinctly smarter.

Antonia phoned on Saturday morning and suggested they met at the restaurant at eight.

'Reggiori's, in Euston Road, practically opposite St Pancras, darling. It's my regular haunt, red plush and brass, suits me down to the ground, terribly decadent, but the

159

food is as good as you'll get anywhere. Can you make it, or would you like me to collect you?'

'That won't be necessary.'

'Reggiori's at eight, then.'

'Antonia . . .'

'What, darling?'

'Will Hector be there?'

'God, yes. I haven't bumped him off yet.'

The fine silk stirred against her skin as she moved. She'd made French knickers and a slip and trimmed them with the lace. To complete the ensemble, she was wearing the one pair of nylons she owned. Over it all, she had the severe black suit with the false shirt front she'd worn for the inquest. And her soon-to-be-discarded tweed coat.

She left the house about twenty to eight with the intention of walking along to Vauxhall Bridge Road and finding a taxi. First, her attention was caught by the road safety poster opposite. Something else had been added to it. She crossed the street. They'd carefully coloured the widow's face, giving her lipstick, rouge and mascara. The eyes were now light blue. The falling tear had been blocked out entirely. If not a merry widow, she was certainly less bleak than before.

Rose smiled at her.

16

REGGIORI'S must have been a cleaner's nightmare. Ornate fittings in abundance: the original gas jets, hat pegs, doorknobs, hand rails and bar furniture. More brass than the Royal Philharmonic. Red plush settees, wall mirrors, mosaic floor, ornamental tiles, potted ferns and silver cruets.

Antonia waved from a table against the wall and Hector stood up and helped Rose into her chair. Whatever it was on his hair smelt expensive. She smiled her thanks. The guarded look he gave her in return was difficult to understand. He'd been so open the last time they had met.

After they'd ordered, Antonia asked about the funeral and Rose told her how Rex Ballard, Peter Bliss and the others had driven down from Kettlesham Heath. 'I wasn't too happy about them coming at first, but as it turned out they helped me get through the day.'

Ridges of tension showed in Antonia's cheek. 'You didn't mention my name?'

'No, I didn't.'

'Did they?'

'No.'

The lines softened and disappeared. 'I expect they were shocked about Barry.'

'Rex could hardly take it in.'

'I bet he wasn't lost for words, though.'

Rose smiled. 'No.'

The wine waiter arrived and Hector asked whether Rose cared for Italian wine. She made the mistake of asking if wine wasn't rather extravagant and got ticked off by Antonia.

'The war's over now. You've got to get out of that scrimp-and-save mentality.'

'People in your circumstances can. It's not so easy for the rest of us.'

'Oh, send me to the guillotine, darling. I don't know how the poor live.'

Hector turned from ordering the wine and showed that he had missed the point entirely. 'I think in this country they don't use the guillotine.' He made a 'V' shape between thumb and forefinger of his right hand and pressed it hard into the angle of his neck and jaw, at the same time pulling an imaginery lever with his left hand. He

162

ended the performance by giving a doglike stare at Rose that made her feel extremely uneasy.

She took a sip of water and tried to think of some other topic, but Antonia was unaffected.

'I see that our ex-RAF colleague went to the scaffold this morning.'

'Oh?'

'Neville Heath.'

Rose tensed. Hector made a vibrating sound with his lips but it didn't discourage Antonia.

'According to the *Star*, he took leave of the world in style. They asked for his last request and he said he'd like a whisky. When it was handed to him and everyone was waiting he said, "I think I'll make that a double." Nice sense of humour.'

Rose said, 'I can't admire a man who did the things he did. Can we change the subject?'

'If you like, darling. What shall we talk about—carburettors? No, Hector, it's meant to be a joke, like the double whisky.'

Hector didn't talk about carburettors. He told them he'd spent another good day at the Victoria & Albert Museum, where his refrigerator was being demonstrated at the Britain

163

Can Make It exhibition. Crowds had formed every day around the stand and there was tremendous interest from retailers.

'How thrilling for you! I must come and see it.'

His chestnut eyes suddenly shone again. 'You tell me when. I can get you in complimentary.'

Antonia studied her fingernails. 'Don't get carried away, Rosie. Just about everything in that tinpot exhibition is marked "For export only", including his precious fridge.'

Hector glared at her.

The minestrone made a timely arrival. Rose took a first spoonful, watched by Antonia.

'Good?'

'This wasn't out of a tin.'

'Did your parents come up for the funeral?'

'Yes. They asked me to go home with them.'

'Why? Do they need looking after?'

'They were thinking of me.'

'You're lucky. They must be fond of you. My mother's impossible. Even Hector can't stand her.'

'Not true, Antonia.'

'Oh, get away with you, Hec. You complained of a headache last time and we had to leave early.' She picked up a slice of bread and started picking it to pieces. Rose, as she listened, quickly sensed that Antonia was at it again, manipulating people, but this time Hector seemed to be the target. 'This is fearfully boring for you, Rosie, but now that the subject of Ma has come up, I've got something to ask my husband. I had a letter from home this morning, dearest. It's about Lucky.'

Hector frowned. 'Lucky?'

'The dog, you chump.' She sighed and turned to Rose. 'If ever an animal was mis-named, it's this one. Ma collected it from the dogs' home when I was still a school-girl, that's how old it is. It was blind in one eye and she felt sorry for it. A cross between a bull terrier and a Bedlington, if you can imagine that. Pink eyes and white woolly hair. It's been run over twice and has a metal splint in one leg. One of its ears was torn off in a fight and it went deaf in the air raids. Lucky!'

Hector nodded. 'First time I met this Lucky, he make water on my new shoes.'

'Thank you, dear heart. The dog has an unreliable bladder to add to its miseries and Ma's, but I wasn't going to speak of it over dinner. The latest bulletin is that it's developed a chronic case of mange. The woolly coat is dropping like snow all over the house. Ma says she must face the inevitable.'

'He must go?'

'Poor old thing, yes. What's that song of Gracie Fields?—"Wish Me Luck as You Wave Me Goodbye".—The thing is, she can't bear the thought of taking the old dog to the vet, so she wants me to go up there and do the necessary.'

Hector's eyebrows pricked up. 'Kill it?'

'Pass it over to the vet. She's in a frightful state about it.'

He lifted his shoulders and spread his hands. 'You'd better go, then.'

'But it's bound to mean two or three days away. Apart from all that travelling, I'm going to have a distraught mother to deal with.' She hesitated before asking Hector in a voice pitched on a tragic note, 'I suppose you won't come with me?'

Rose sipped her soup and looked into the mid-distance. She wished Antonia had saved this conversation for later.

Hector shook his head. 'Britain Can Make It.'

'So Hector obviously can't. No, I don't mean to be rude. I shall just have to go on my own. You *do* understand that the doggie has to be dealt with, Hec, my pet?'

Antonia's concern for her husband was as warming as it was unexpected. A pity she called him her 'pet' in the circumstances, but he seemed not to take it badly.

He leaned towards Rose. 'My wife, she is highly suitable for such a sad duty. No nerves. No panics.'

'I can believe it.'

The matter still wasn't settled to Antonia's satisfaction, even though Hector had given his blessing. There was the problem of his eating arrangements. 'How can I go up to Manchester knowing you won't eat a thing? It's no good looking at me like that, Hector. You're too proud to eat in a restaurant alone.'

He shook his head. 'Not too proud. I don't enjoy it, that's all.'

'It comes down to the same thing.' She swung round and addressed Rose. 'You see how difficult he makes it? The silly man won't have a hot dinner for as long as I'm gone.'

'How does he manage for lunch?'

'Never eats it. This is the only substantial meal he gets. He's going to collapse if he doesn't eat something.'

The thought crossed Rose's mind that if

all Hector was lacking was a dining companion, she could easily volunteer. This thought was overtaken by another: this concern for Hector's eating arrangements didn't square with Antonia's plans for him. No, she thought. Something lies behind this.

She slipped in a suggestion. 'Couldn't you cook something like a stew before you go and leave it in the oven for Hector to warm up?'

As if Hector hadn't heard of anything so humble as stew, Antonia provided a rough translation. 'Goulash.'

He gave a shrug.

'Darling, he'd like nothing better, but there are two little snags. First, I couldn't make a stew to save my life, and second, Hector would blow up the house trying to light the gas.'

'Could I do it?'

'Light the gas?'

'Prepare the evening meal.' The suggestion came from Rose spontaneously, and immediately after making it she cursed herself for being so impetuous. Then she thought about the prospect more calmly and decided that if Antonia were away in Manchester there couldn't be any harm in it. She'd do as much for any friend. It was a practical and agreeable way of dispensing at least a little of the obligation she had to Antonia. 'I can easily cook up a stew, but I don't know about goulash.'

'It's just extra seasoning, like curry. That's a thought!' Antonia smiled knowingly at Hector and he nodded back.

Rose looked towards each of them in turn. 'What's that?'

'Could you make a curry for him? He'd adore that.'

She liked the suggestion. It would be much more tempting to serve up to Hector than plain old stew. 'Well, yes. I make quite a passable lamb curry.'

'Darling, that's awfully good of you. Let me buy the ingredients. The meat. Everything. It'll keep in the fridge. We'll give you a key and you can let yourself in whenever you want and do the cooking. Hector gets home about six from the exhibition. He won't be a minute late if there's a curry waiting. You're an angel.'

Hector raised his glass to her. 'The lady who is about to save my life.'

She felt herself go pink.

At the door of Reggiori's, Antonia was handed a box not unlike the cake-box she'd picked up at the Ritz. Rose asked what the cat was getting for supper and learned that it was salmon.

They drove her back to Pimlico in the Bentley. She thanked them profusely for the meal and for bringing her home.

While Hector was turning the car she stood waving from her front door.

'Like some little girl who went to a birth-day party.'

'What?' Antonia was staring out of the other window at the road safety poster.

'Rosie. Such nice manners. I believe you're wrong about her. She wouldn't make trouble for us with the police. Didn't you see how she really wants to cook dinner for me? She jumped at it. How can you think of this wicked thing?'

'Don't start up now, little man. I'm pooped.'

'Pooped from telling so many lies.'

Hector wasn't used to getting the last word, so it was no surprise when Antonia pitched in as they were motoring up Park Lane. 'She really took you in, didn't she? You're a sucker for the little-girl-lost look. The timid smile and watery blue eyes.'

'No wonder her eyes are sad when her husband just died. Don't you have no pity?'

Antonia shook with amusement, taking gusts of air through her nostrils. 'You prize idiot! She isn't suffering. Barry was no loss. She killed him.'

He drew the car in to the kerb and switched off the engine. 'Antonia, I do not believe this.'

'He was a washout as a husband so she shoved him on to the Piccadilly Line and picked up five thousand in insurance. Don't waste any sympathy on Rose Bell, my innocent. She's a killer. You can ask her.'

'How can I ask such a thing?'

'Ask her if she really misses him. You'll see the guilt in her face.'

17

Rose used a key Antonia had given her to enter the house in Park Crescent early on Tuesday afternoon. Antonia had phoned that morning to say she was catching the 11.25 from Euston, adding that she'd stocked up at Fortnum's and a little place she knew that didn't bother with ration books and she'd left heaps of things in the fridge and Rose was to use whatever she wanted and to hell with austerity.

Until the moment the latch clicked behind her, Rose hadn't foreseen the unease she would feel letting herself into someone else's house. All five doors leading off from the hall were closed. She wished she'd been more observant of the layout when Antonia had brought her here before, instead of goggling at it all like a GI in Piccadilly Circus. She did remember that the blue and white sitting room looked on to the street, so presumably that was the first door, but which was the kitchen? Somewhere ahead. She stepped forward, grasped a handle, turned it and found herself staring into darkness. Judging by the musty smell, it was the route to the cellar.

She closed that door and tried another. Second time lucky. Hector's enormous fridge gave a welcoming throb. She slipped off her coat and hung it on a hook behind the door.

There was a folded note on the kitchen table with her name on it. Antonia's writing was huge. It ran to several sheets.

Rose Darling,
  You're one in a million.
  Meat in the fridge. Also butter and as many fresh veggies as I could carry home. Onions on the windowsill. Raisins and

172

sultanas in the canisters on the dresser (second shelf) next to all the spices. Be generous with the curry powder—Hec doesn't believe it's the real thing unless he breathes fire after it. Oh, and if you want to go to the trouble of rice, there's a packet beside the breadbin. Hope I haven't forgotten anything essential. Found the ingredients in the New World cookery book, which I'm sure you won't need to use—I've never used it either!

Hec says he will be in about six each night and for once he definitely means it.

Raffles will finish any trimmings from the meat. Did I mention that he's the cat?

I'm counting on being back by Saturday. Let's all have another meal at Reggiori's. By God, you deserve it!

Love,
Antonia

It was a good thing that Raffles was mentioned, because before Rose had finished reading the note she felt a movement against her leg. A second or two earlier and neither she nor the cat would have got much pleasure from the contact. She picked him up and faced the scrutiny of his large orange eyes.

'So you're Raffles, are you? Shall we see if we can crack this safe together? Oh, my word, look at this!'

A family could have fed from that fridge for a month. She put Raffles down and collected butter and lard by the armful just to find a way through to the milk.

Having filled the cat's saucer she went back to the fridge. Presently she located the meat—beautiful boned lamb and heaps more than she needed for a single curry, whatever the capacity of Hector's appetite. She picked a large piece that must have weighed two pounds or so, then looked round for a knife and chopping board. She was going to need extra time for working in a strange kitchen.

Everything she required was somewhere nearby, only had to be found first. It took the best part of an hour to collect all the ingredients, chop the meat and onion and take it through the frying stage, but she got engrossed in the cooking and didn't fret about the time.

She hadn't felt so pleased to be preparing food for months. Cooking lost its appeal when your husband told you frankly that he regarded eating as 'stoking up'. Barry would have cheerfully stoked up every day with baked beans if they were put in front of him. It wasn't as if Rose hadn't tried to educate his taste. Time and again, notwithstanding rationing and shortages, she'd put some special dish on the table after queuing and cooking most of the day only to see him bolt it without looking up from the evening paper.

She stirred in two tablespoonfuls of curry powder, enough, she decided, to produce the strong curry Hector expected without altogether masking the other spices, for she'd found ginger, garlic and paprika lined up on the dresser. Raisins, sliced celery and chopped apple and tomato went into the pot to simmer with the meat until it was tender. Reggiori's had better watch out!

By then it was getting on for half past four. She washed up and thought about setting the table. It ought to be ready for when he came in. Where was the dining room, she wondered. She didn't want her famous curry to be eaten off the kitchen table.

She dried her hands and went to explore. She felt she'd earned the right to try those doors in the hall.

As she switched on a light she gave a cry, half admiring, half envious. A spacious, beautifully proportioned room, cream and pale green, with an oval table that could have seated a dozen easily and still didn't dominate. A fire had been laid in the grate, so she put a match to it and watched it take. Then she went to the windows and drew the curtains. They were ivory-coloured velvet and they skimmed the floor.

She found silver cutlery, placemats and napkins in the top drawer of a mahogany sideboard opposite the fireplace. Like the cooking implements, they'd not been given much use.

It was while she was setting the place for Hector that she had a paralysing thought: why was she putting out a dessert spoon? There was nothing to follow. She'd been so absorbed in preparing the curry that she hadn't given a thought to the rest of the meal.

There *had* to be some form of dessert, but what? There wasn't much time. What would be acceptable after a piping hot curry? Something moist. Fruit? After all the trouble she'd taken with the first course it would be a dreadful letdown just to open a tin of peaches.

A fresh fruit salad would be better. Coming out of Regent's Park tube station on the way to Antonia's she'd passed a stall selling apples and pears and there had been hardly any queue to speak of.

She looked at the time, shovelled some more coal on the fire and collected her coat.

On the way she thought of something better. There was a story her mother delighted in telling about the evening Daddy had thrown his annual dinner party at the rectory for the church wardens and their wives. It had always been a staid affair. That year Mummy had found a recipe for pears poached in red wine which proved to be such a success that two or three of the guests had become merry after second helpings. When they'd all tottered out at the end of the evening, Daddy had asked what the recipe was called. Mummy had given an innocent smile and said, 'Wardens in Wine'. A warden, she'd discovered, was an old English name for a pear used in cooking.

She'd noticed several bottles of Burgundy lying on their sides on the floor of the larder. If there were any pears left on the greengrocer's stall, her problem would be solved.

Although it was almost dark, the man was still there, working under an electric light bulb. Rose bought three large Comice pears. Twenty-five past five. Ten minutes, preparation and twenty for the poaching. She could just get everything done in time.

The simmering curry was giving off a rich aroma when Rose got back to the house. She checked that the fire was burning well in the dining room and then set to work in the kitchen. While she was peeling and coring the pears, her thoughts returned to Antonia. How odd that any woman equipped with this dream of a kitchen could take no interest in cooking. Terribly sad, really, that Hector devoted his working life to manufacturing labour-saving machines for women and was married to someone who didn't appreciate them in the slightest. Perhaps Antonia should have employed a cook. Well, she has, in a way, Rose thought, smiling. I'm in service here. I'm not doing it from altruism. I'm under an obligation to her; she killed my husband, so I cook for hers when she goes away. Not a bad division of responsibility from my point of view.

In fact, I'm enjoying it. It must be years since I had such a satisfying afternoon.

It was too bad that oranges were still blue books only. A few thin strips of peel would have completed the dish. At least there was spice. She added sugar and a few cloves.

Then she brought it all to the boil and let it simmer.

Time to heat some water for the rice.

I wonder if Antonia has any idea what a treat this is for me. Or, come to that, what a treat is in store for Hector. To be fair, she provided all the ingredients. That meat is superb. It smells delicious.

She's so inconsistent, talking to me about wanting to do away with Hector, and then going to no end of trouble to see that he's properly fed.

Unless . . .

Unless I've totally misunderstood what's going on.

Please God, no!

She's capable of it.

She knows I'd refuse point blank if she asked me to administer poison to her husband. But what if I'm unaware of what I'm doing?

'Be generous with the curry powder.'

Curry will mask the taste of arsenic or strychnine or whatever she managed to obtain from her boyfriend Vic, the chemistry lecturer. The plan is horribly clear. She went to her mother to give herself an alibi. In my ignorance I'm about to serve up a poisoned curry for Hector and kill him. When she comes back from Manchester she'll fill in the blank death certificate and have him cremated.

Or am I imagining this?

He'll be here any minute.

18

HECTOR opened the kitchen door and looked in. His eyes lit up when he saw her and he gave a huge sigh of relief, almost as if he'd expected somebody else to be there.

'Smells nice.'

'Please ignore the smell.'

'Why?'

'I'm sorry. There won't be any curry after all.'

He gave a gurgle of amusement. He was going out of his way to be pleasant. 'It's done. I can smell it. Where is it?'

'It's gone.'

'Gone? Gone where?'

'Down the toilet.'

'Is this a joke, Rosie? You wouldn't make fun of me?'

'It was a bad curry. You couldn't possibly have eaten it. I'm going to try and do something else instead. It won't take long, I promise. Do you like omelettes?'

'Please—my curry—what went wrong?'

He put it to her with good-natured concern, as if enquiring after the health of a friend. Rose felt compelled to give him an answer. What she told him, however, was a lie. If he was convinced that his wife had set a trap to poison him, he'd go straight to the police. Even if he was unconvinced, he would want an explanation. As sure as God made little apples, the truth about Barry would come out.

She did her best to make it plausible. 'I suppose I was nervous. Something went wrong in the cooking.'

'You burnt it?'

'Not exactly.'

'I can't smell burning.'

'No. It was what went into it. The ingredients. They weren't right. I'd like to try again tomorrow, if you'll allow me. I'll get it right next time. Now will you please let me cook you an omelette or a fried egg or something?'

His eyes had a sceptical glint. He crossed the room to the sink and ran his forefinger around the inner side of the saucepan Rose had half-filled with water.

She moved fast. She reached out to him and grasped his sleeve. 'Don't!'

'You don't let me taste? Not even taste?'

She snatched up a teacloth and wiped his finger clean. 'Not even taste.'

He laughed and took a grip on her hand through the towel and squeezed it. She had her back to the draining board so she couldn't easily move.

'You know what I think you are, Rosie— apart from Antonia's best friend?'

Her neck and shoulders tensed. She was suddenly convinced that he'd misinterpreted her actions and was about to make a pass. She was in no state to deal with it. She swayed back and took a shallow, rasping breath.

His hand darted to her face and lightly pinched the point of her chin. 'A fusspot. A proper little fusspot.'

It was embarrassing on both sides. Faced with her jittery reaction he'd fallen back on a fatuous gesture and the sort of silly, doting thing said by middle-aged men to their simpering wives. He must have felt it as acutely as she, because he backed off at once.

Rose turned to the sink and made a performance of wiping the saucepan clean as her mind raced. Perhaps she'd been mistaken. Perhaps he'd only meant to make light of the problem over the curry. He'd responded to her state of nerves by touching her. It was innocent, a spontaneous gesture.

When Hector's voice came again it was from a safe distance. 'I'll make a bargain with you, Rosie. You cook me curry tomorrow. Tonight I will take you to Reggiori's.'

She looked across the table at him. He was still wearing his camelhair overcoat and he'd picked up his porkpie hat. 'I couldn't possibly.'

'One little mistake in the cooking and you lose your confidence? This is not good, Rosie.'

'I'll make the curry. I said I would. What I mean is that I couldn't under any circumstances go out to dinner with you.' She turned to face him across the table. 'It's not the right way to behave, you see. I can't be seen having dinner with someone else's husband.'

'You did the other night.'

'Antonia was with us.'

'So the people in Reggiori's know it's all right. Rosie is Antonia's friend, not Hector's lover.'

She felt the colour spread across her face.

Mortifying. 'Please allow me to cook you something else.'

'Not possible.' He was adamant, like a chess-player who knew he had mate in three. 'I had no lunch today.'

'No lunch. But why?'

'Antonia told you. I never eat lunch. Only this meal. Now I need—how do you say?—a square meal. Not omelette.'

'Anything else would take hours to prepare.'

'Not at Reggiori's.'

She *couldn't*. What sort of woman would dine in public with a married man the week after she'd buried her husband? It would be deplorable. Yet she felt piercingly guilty for depriving Hector of the meal he'd looked forward to eating. The possibility had to be faced that she'd been mistaken about the poison and thrown away a perfectly good meal. And she knew Hector objected to going to restaurants alone; it wasn't some stratagem he'd just thought up. It was her whole justification for being here.

He lifted her coat off the hook on the back of the door. 'All right, Rosie. Please forget what I said. I will take you home now.'

She was caught off guard. 'Where will you eat?'

He gave a shrug. 'I don't know. I don't intend to starve. I will come home, look in the fridge, make myself a sandwich.'

From the fridge. 'No.'

He arched his eyebrows.

She had a picture of him opening the fridge and finding the rest of the meat, or something else that Antonia had laced with poison. 'I've changed my mind.'

He thoughtfully suggested they sit at a table for four rather than one of the more intimate doubles. To anyone interested it must have seemed that they expected to be joined by the rest of their party later.

'You look nervous, Rosie.'

'I am, a little.'

'You want some wine?'

'No, thank you.'

'Not many people are here so early as you and me.'

'No.'

'That's good?'

'Yes.'

He made a noble effort to be entertaining, talking of the gadgets he'd seen at the exhibition and the way women's lives would soon be transformed. For a man, he had some revolutionary ideas. Most women would have thought of them as mutinous. He talked about the drudgery of housework and rejected the idea that it was a proof of virtue. 'All that scrubbing of doorsteps. What for? So that all the neighbours will say she's a good woman like us, scrubs her step every day. Rosie, very soon all those good women will get red hands and lumpy knees. Don't be like that.'

She smiled faintly. 'What should I do, then—buy one of your machines? Do you supply a doorstep-scrubbing machine?'

'No. There is no market for such a machine. Simply forget about your doorstep.'

'And have all my neighbours think I'm a slut?'

'The women maybe. Men think something else. What nice legs this lady has.'

She looked primly down at her plate. Being foreign, he may not have appreciated how personal some of his remarks appeared.

'It's true. You have legs like Betty Grable's. Better.'

'I'm sure you mean it kindly, but I wish you'd talk about something else.'

'Not your legs?'

'Not my legs.'

'Your chest?'

Her arm jerked and she spilled some soup. She picked her napkin off her lap and rearranged it, trying frantically to think of something to divert him from this tack. 'I wonder if Antonia will telephone you tonight.'

'Excuse me, Rosie. My English. I don't think you understand. I said "chest". Is it more suitable to say "chests"?'

'It's unsuitable however you say it. Perhaps she telephoned you earlier? I dare say she would want you to know she'd arrived safely.'

'I am so sorry. I think I embarrass you with my bad grammar.'

'It's not the grammar.'

'You don't think so?'

'It's the personal things you mention.'

'I understand. I think I mean bust. Can I say you have a pretty fine bust?'

Through iron persistence she succeeded at length in directing his thoughts to Antonia. It appeared that he didn't expect a phone call. They didn't phone each other unless it was necessary. They had nothing to say to each other. 'Antonia, she doesn't understand me.'

'Oh, yes?' Rose kept her response as bland

as possible. Of all the come-ons men resorted to, that was the corniest.

He tried to do better. 'She has a friend. A man friend. You know?'

'It's none of my business.'

'This friend is off to America soon. Nice new job. Princeton University. Antonia wants to go with him.'

'Mm?'

'Yes. It's true. You can ask her.'

'I wouldn't dream of asking her a thing like that.'

'Antonia and me, we sleep single.'

Opportunely the arrival of the main course foreclosed discussion of the sleeping arrangements. Hector had ordered Dover sole in breadcrumbs, which he explained wouldn't spoil his appetite for the curry Rose had promised for the next evening. She didn't want to be reminded about tomorrow. Getting through the present evening without misunderstanding was as much as she could cope with.

He gave her the cue for a more congenial line of conversation. 'So you were one of the WAAFs, like Antonia?'

'Yes. At Kettlesham Heath. I expect she's told you about it many times.'

'But I would like to hear from you. What did you do?'

'I was a plotter, like Antonia. In an underground control room. Very hush-hush. We had to sign a paper promising not to say anything about our work.'

He seemed to find this amusing. 'Ladies talk so much they can't keep no secret.'

'You're mistaken. We're much more discreet than the average man.'

'Yes?' He gave her a silly grin and she almost lost patience with him. His own life was threatened and he was so complacent that he hadn't a hope of finding out.

'Take Antonia. She's much more guarded than you appreciate. If she has a reason to keep something to herself, nothing will drag it from her.'

'You think?'

'I'm certain.'

His expression changed. 'Rosie, you are right about Antonia. She is a plotter still.'

She hesitated. He was an eager listener and she was on the brink of saying too much. 'Most of us women have our secret hopes and plans, if that's what you mean. Anyway, I was telling you about Kettlesham Heath. It was demanding work—sheer hell sometimes —and we couldn't afford to make mistakes.

Actually Antonia was the most reliable of all the girls on watch. She didn't get tense. She could talk and joke and keep everyone smiling and never lose her concentration.'

'She was popular?'

'Certainly.'

'Plenty of officers went out with her. It's all right, she told me this.'

'Well, yes.'

'And you, Rosie? Did you have plenty?'

She allowed herself to smile. 'I wouldn't describe it in quite those terms. I wasn't so popular as Antonia. If I'd been asked I'd have gone out with almost any officer with wings. Any of us would. It was a question of prestige. Good looks and age came a long way after rank. They had to have stripes on their sleeves and the more the better. Funny, isn't it? There were some good-looking fellows among the sergeant pilots, but to go out with them was slumming. It was the service mentality, I suppose. Silly. I married a wing commander.' She stopped and lowered her eyes. She hadn't wanted to mention Barry.

Anyone with a modicum of tact would have moved to another subject. Hector sat up in his seat and leaned on his elbows and gave her a penetrating stare as if nothing interested him so much. 'Tell me, Rosie, do you miss your husband?'

She frowned. His dark eyes locked with hers and it was almost like being interrogated. She wondered for a petrifying moment if he suspected something. Then with a sense of relief she realized what this was about. How typical of a man, she thought. He thinks I'm on the lookout for someone. How can I possibly convey to him that those stories about freshly widowed women falling for the next man who passes the time of day with them are untrue, quite monstrously untrue?

'I should never have got married.'

'You don't miss him, then?'

'I'd rather talk about something else.'

'Won't you try again?'

'It's most unlikely.'

'You will get lonely.'

'I don't suppose I will.'

'You are very pretty. Some fellow will ask to marry you soon.'

It was a long time since anyone had paid her any kind of compliment. In her situation it was inopportune, but better than an insult. Or an interrogation.

'Shall we look at the menu again?'

He looked mystified. 'I spoke something wrong?'

It might have been uncharitable, but she had a suspicion that Hector was overplaying the part of the foreigner baffled by English. He'd lived in America and England for fifteen years or so and must have used the language pretty effectively to earn the money he had.

They decided to have coffee instead of desserts. He offered her a liqueur. She thanked him and said no, adding that she didn't want to stop him from having one. She smoked a cigarette while he had a brandy. She needed the smoke. She'd staunched the flow of personal remarks, but she felt uneasy. His eyes never left hers. She didn't know if it was her imagination or if he was planning something.

As they were collecting their coats, he suggested she waited inside the restaurant while he fetched the car, which he'd parked in a side street.

'That isn't necessary. I'll take the tube from here. The meal was delicious. Thank you.' She thrust her arms into the coat and made a decisive move towards the door. 'I'll see you tomorrow.'

'Rosie!' He caught up with her outside

and clutched her arm to restrain her. 'I said I will drive you.'

'No, thank you.'

'Excuse me, but why not?'

She was flustered, so the words that came out sounded more ungrateful than she intended. 'You wanted a meal and I came with you out of politeness. Now would you please let go of my arm?'

He walked beside her as she set off smartly along Euston Road. 'Please, did I say something wrong tonight?'

'You're making this very difficult.'

'I cannot allow this, Rosie.'

'Hector, I'm not your property.'

This had a startling effect. He flung up his arms as if in surrender. 'Forgive me. I should never have said such things. You are Antonia's friend. You come specially to my house to cook a nice meal for me. What disgusting manners I have!'

They'd reached a street corner and had to stop for the traffic. Some people standing there had picked up Hector's last remark and turned round. He must have seemed comical making an exhibition of himself in his expensive overcoat and porkpie hat. Rose didn't find it amusing.

She made a sideward step and tried to

give the impression she was unaccompanied. Hector didn't move. He simply raised his voice. 'Please forgive me. Allow me to be a gentleman and drive you safe home.'

She looked to right and left, hoping to God that the underground sign was somewhere about. An elderly couple had joined the group at the curb. The woman was trying to prompt Rose by nodding and smiling.

Hector was oblivious of his audience. 'Don't go down the tube, Rosie.'

It was like an echo of the old tear-jerking ballad 'Don't go down the mine, Daddy'. Ludicrous. This could only get more embarrassing. He wouldn't give up. And she didn't want it to end in a blazing row.

She spun around. 'All right. Which way is the car?'

After all, she'd made her point. He could be in no doubt now that she wanted him to remain at arm's length.

During the drive to Oldfield Gardens Hector behaved impeccably. He was charming and witty. He talked glowingly of the curry she had promised him the next day and how in order to put his mind at rest he planned to lock the toilet door and hide the key. She took it in good part and said she could think of dozens of ways of dispos-

ing of a curry and some of them were very
messy indeed, so he'd better leave the toilet
open and trust his luck and hers.

'This your street, Rosie?'

'Yes, don't you remember? The house at
the end, opposite the hoarding.'

He drew in and braked.

She turned and leaned back slightly in the
same movement to keep her face out of range.
'Thank you. It was a splendid meal.'

'Only second best.'

'Perhaps.'

'We'll find out tomorrow, eh?'

'If you're still willing to risk it. Hector . . . ?'

'Yes?'

'There is still some meat in the fridge.
You won't use any, will you?'

'You think I want to cook a midnight
feast? Without anyone to share?'

'I just wanted to mention it.'

He laughed softly. 'Rosie, believe me, I
don't touch nothing.'

She opened the car door, profoundly relieved at getting home without incident. On
an impulse she reached out and put her hand
over his, squeezing his fingers slightly. 'Tomorrow, then.'

19

THAT night Rose had an inspiration. A stunning solution to all the problems. She was certain it would work.

To tell it right, the idea didn't come in a blinding flash. She came to it through a process that started the moment she left Hector.

Her first thought after watching the Bentley turn in the road and sweep out of Oldfield Gardens was that she'd made a perfect fool of herself. She should never have squeezed his hand like some schoolgirl on a blind date.

She closed her front door and leaned against it with her hands clasped against the back of her neck and her eyes pressed shut and played the scene in her mind again, trying to see it from Hector's point of view. He could have taken the gesture as what it was, a clumsy attempt to show she had his welfare at heart in spite of the hard time she'd given him. Or, more alarmingly, as a promise of passion. How she wished she hadn't added that, 'Tomorrow, then.'

Maybe he'd already dismissed the whole thing from his mind.

She considered this a moment and discovered that it wasn't the comfort it should have been. Deep down, she hoped he hadn't treated the incident as unimportant. For all Hector's hair-raising remarks, he was a stimulating companion. And he gave you his total attention.

How Antonia could contemplate killing him was beyond belief. There was no question that she meant to do it. She'd got the death certificate ready. She'd talked about having him cremated. He was doomed. He might have been dying in agony at this minute if he'd eaten that curry.

Rose started to shake. She went through to the kitchen and opened the larder and saw the space on the shelf where the brandy had been. She gave a moan as she remembered smashing the bottle.

A cigarette, then. She found the packet and her lighter and sat at the kitchen table taking quick, shallow puffs, unable any longer to shut out the horror of what was happening.

No wonder she was in a state. She was

poleaxed by the conviction that she had come so close to poisoning Hector. And angry at her own stupidity and Antonia's deceit. Above all, she was frightened.

If Hector had died and his murder had been discovered, Antonia, up in Manchester, would have had a convincing alibi. The prime suspect would have been Rose herself.

She winced, as if the pain were physical. As a schemer Antonia was in a class of her own. She had planned from the beginning to use her. There was a price to be paid for Barry's death. It was naïve in the extreme to suppose the favour could be repaid by cooking a few meals for Hector. He was down to be murdered.

'Not by me,' she said aloud. 'There was never any suggestion of that. *Never.*'

Antonia seemed to think nothing of killing people. She'd pushed Barry under the train without turning a hair. She'd contrived to have Hector poisoned while she went to visit her mother. And—Rose shuddered as she remembered—she'd talked of waiting for Hector's first wife to die—by drowning. At the time it had seemed incomprehensible. Not now.

Pull yourself together and be positive, Rose told herself. How stupid of Antonia to think that the answer to every problem is murder. Hector's only offence is that he won't give her a divorce. Surely they can end their unhappy marriage in some other way?

She drew more deeply on the cigarette.

Then the inspiration dawned.

If Hector won't give Antonia a divorce because he's a Roman Catholic, why shouldn't *she* divorce him? If he's the guilty party Antonia can take her case to court and win. She can have a share of his fortune, which she's after, and she'll be free to marry Vic.

Above all, Hector's life will be saved.

Her mouth went dry as she pursued the idea. On what grounds could Antonia divorce him? Cruelty? That won't wash. Desertion? Definitely not. Insanity? No. Failure to consummate? Unlikely.

That left adultery. Antonia had brushed aside the possibility of other women. *'No vultures circling overhead. I'd know.'*

In that case Hector has to be persuaded to take a lover.

Rose plunged a hand into her hair and gripped it hard at the roots.

It has to be me.

I can't, she thought. Jesus Christ, it's only three weeks since my husband died. I'm a widow. I don't love Hector. I've met him on three occasions. I've never been so embarrassed as when he made that pass at me in the kitchen and ended up calling me a fusspot. I don't find him attractive.

Do I?

No use questioning my motives. Suddenly to be taken out for a meal after five years of being ignored is quite head-turning, but that doesn't come into it. I wouldn't dream of going to bed with Hector. Not unless everything altered and made it possible, anyway. And then not for many months . . . .

I must get this clear in my mind. I won't be doing it for any other reason than necessity, to save him from being murdered, and myself from worse trouble than I'm in already.

She felt groggy. That brandy would have been a lifesaver at this minute. There was some ginger wine somewhere in the front room. She collected it and poured herself a large glass.

I'll be the 'other woman' in a divorce case. Horrible. It's sure to be in the newspapers. Mummy and Daddy will get to hear of it. They don't read the gutter press, but plenty of people in the parish do. A divorce scandal is the very thing I was so desperate to avoid.

I had Barry killed because I wouldn't divorce him.

Oh, God, what's the alternative? Hector will be killed. He's a decent man, utterly different from Barry. He takes a pride in his work. He treats me as if I'm a member of the same species, not some lower order. He made a terrible mistake when he fell under Antonia's charm, but I can understand exactly how it happened. Knowing the force of Antonia's personality, I can't believe Hector had any part in his first wife's death. He obviously misses her. He must have been rushed into marrying Antonia when he was most vulnerable.

Killing him would be wicked. Indefensible. Yet Antonia will find some way of doing it, with my help or without. She wants him dead. And if she's arrested, one thing is certain. She'll name me as her accomplice.

What it comes down to is the lesser of two evils. What would you rather have your daughter be, Daddy—an adulteress or a murderess?

She lit another cigarette.

If only there were more time. To be any use at all, the thing had to be accomplished before Antonia returned from Manchester. She would come back expecting to find Hector dead. Instead, she would be handed the alternative—an admission of his adultery.

She reached for the bottle again.

How soon, then?

Tomorrow.

With an effort to suppress her fears she gave some thought to the practicality of getting Hector into bed. Or getting into bed with Hector. She didn't think of it as seducing him. If she'd read the signals right, he wouldn't need much prompting. She hadn't forgotten how he'd squeezed her hand in the kitchen at Park Crescent, or how he'd made her blush with his personal remarks in Reggiori's. He was a foreigner, yes, and they got into muddles sometimes, but to say she had legs as good as Betty Grable's and a 'pretty fine bust' couldn't be put down to faulty syntax.

She could cook a tempting meal, anyway. She'd cook that curry to perfection and serve it with a bottle of Burgundy. Then a spectacular dessert was wanted: why not peach melba?

With the menu decided, she let her thoughts creep ahead. I have set a place for Hector at the oval table in the dining room. Before he eats he invites me to join him, but I insist with a demure smile that I have come there only to cook. I serve the meal and leave him to savour every delicious mouthful, telling him I have things to attend to in the kitchen. I wash the dishes and the pans and leave everything in immaculate condition.

Then I offer him coffee.

I ask how he likes it, and he doggedly says he would like it best if I will drink it with him. I weigh the suggestion solemnly and say instead that if he is kind enough to drive me back to Pimlico I'll make coffee for both of us there.

So I show him into the front room at Oldfield Gardens, where the fire glows warmly. I go to the kitchen to make the coffee. Presently I call out casually that if he looks in the sideboard he'll find a bottle of champagne and two glasses waiting.

The train of thought stopped abruptly. She flinched at the prospect of sex with Hector. She hadn't even kissed him up to now. True, she wasn't without experience, but compared with Antonia . . . .

She shivered.

She would see how she felt in the morning.

20

FROST-PATTERNS had formed on the inside of the bedroom windows. She scraped away a section to see if it was foggy outside and saw the words 'Carelessness Kills'.

A superfluous warning. She had already decided to buy fresh ingredients for the curry, regardless that the lamb alone would use up all her meat ration for that week. She couldn't believe it was possible for Antonia to have introduced poison into the vegetables, but just to be certain she would buy them fresh. Plus curry powder, which certainly couldn't be left to chance.

She was first in the queue for the butcher's when he opened at 8.30.

'Yes, for you, as it happens, I do have some prime lamb, Mrs Bell. People coming to stay?'

'Not to stay. Just a meal for a . . . for some friends. People have been very kind to me.'

'Glad to hear it. Does you no harm to have company. Takes your mind off things.'

'I hope so.'

'That's the spirit, my love. Never say die.'

After the grocer's and the greengrocer's she took a bus to Regent's Park and let herself into the house in Park Crescent. It wasn't ten o'clock yet.

She took her shopping into the kitchen and unloaded it on the table. She'd managed to get a brick of Wall's ice cream for the peach melba, so she stacked that with the ice trays in the fridge. The meat also went into the fridge. She took out what was left of the lamb Antonia had supplied, wrapped it in newspaper and stowed it in her shopping basket. The suspect curry powder joined it.

Her reason for coming so early wasn't to do with cooking.

She'd woken about six in a changed mood from the near-panic of the night before. She'd reached a decision. She would search for evidence that Antonia had poisoned Hector's food.

She needed to be certain. Sex with Hector was an alarming prospect but she was prepared to face it if she could find proof that his life was under imminent threat.

She would look for evidence of poison. A good detective would have known what to do. He would have had the food analysed by a toxicologist.

She had to search for the poison itself, or the container it came in.

And (because she really ought to keep an open mind) she would also look for that letter from Antonia's mother. The letter that supposedly summoned Antonia to Manchester to put Lucky the luckless dog out of his misery. She would be surprised if the letter existed. She was pretty certain that these few days of absence had more to do with putting Hector down than Lucky. But she was here to find out the truth.

Might as well start with the obvious and the most unpleasant, she thought. The dustbin. After sifting through muck and rubbish for twenty minutes everything else will be like picking daisies. She opened the back door.

Two dustbins, one empty and the other only half full, thanks to Antonia's dislike of cooking. The smell wasn't as suffocating as it might have been because the contents were mostly dry. She moved them piece by piece into the empty dustbin. The wrapped vegetable parings she had placed in there herself the day before, a pile of newspapers and magazines, a cornflakes carton, a couple of tea packets, several salmon tins (for that pampered cat?), a whisky bottle, a wine bottle, a laddered stocking, cigarette butts and packets, a matchbox, some razor blades, combings of blonde hair, a lipstick holder and some packets of ash and cinders that she unwrapped and sifted with a stick.

She defied the freezing air long enough to check everything again and stack it in the original dustbin.

She came in and ran the hot tap for a wash, glad that the dirtiest job was over and untroubled that it had yielded nothing.

Next on her list was Antonia's dressing room. In a house this size it was inconceivable that Antonia didn't have a room of her own.

The act of going upstairs didn't need to be charged with tension just because it was unexplored territory. She'd made up her mind to treat it casually. On the wall up the staircase there was a collection of framed photographs of allied fighter planes, so she paused to brush up on her aircraft recognition. Nobody likes being alone in a strange house, she told herself, unless like me they're making a search for something.

One of the stairs creaked under her weight and there was an immediate thump from the floor above. She wasn't alarmed for long. The cat came down to meet her at the turn before the next flight. She scratched the top of its head.

'Later. I wouldn't forget you, would I, Raffles?'

She reached the first floor and started opening doors. A study, evidently Hector's, with design drawings on the walls, a roll-top desk and leather furniture. Next to it a library stuffed to the ceiling with technical books in several languages. Then, stale from disuse, a spare room that Antonia would probably have called the glory-hole. Anyone wanting to hide something had unlimited scope in this house. The dressing room was still the likeliest place. She went up to the next floor.

The nearest door was open and she glimpsed two brass bedsteads with a polar bear rug between them, so she went in. The walls were papered in a startling geometric design of overlapping pink arcs and blue triangles, neither restful nor romantic—which summed up Antonia, Rose thought. Hector's pyjamas lay across the black eiderdown on the bed to the right. They were conspicuous, to put it mildly—bright red with white spots that played tricks on the eyes and moved about like the lights in Piccadilly Circus. She refused to believe they were Hector's choice. She put the blame on Antonia again until it occurred to her that they must have come from America, where Hector had lived some years. On second thoughts she decided polka dot pyjamas were like modern paintings. You might very well grow to like them as they became more familiar.

Through the door on the opposite side and into Antonia's dressing room. She got a shock as she met her own reflection in a wall mirror.

White wardrobes with glass handles were built along two walls. She opened a door and gave a long low murmur of envy. She was no authority on furs, but she recognized mink, ocelot, silver fox and chinchilla and plenty she couldn't name but would have gone through fire to wear. A lustrous black coat with raised shoulders and no collar that must have been straight from Paris, it was so fashionable; three or four sensational capes for evening wear; and a heap of tempting hats and collars and things on the shelf above.

She couldn't resist running her fingers through the chinchilla. If I had just one of these I'd be in my seventh heaven, she mused, but *all* of them. Small wonder Antonia refuses to be parted from them.

She wrenched herself away and crossed the room to the walnut dressing table, a long, low arrangement of drawers in a curve with three tall mirrors embellished with Art Deco rosebuds and ribbons. Resisting the temptation to try the spray scents on top, she opened and closed each of the drawers quickly to get an impression of the contents, lingering a moment at the one containing jewellery.

You're here to look for poison, she told herself.

Any time she had reason to hide an article —usually nothing more sinister than a birthday present for Barry—she tucked it among the smalls at the back of her underwear drawer where nobody but herself had any business to look. Here in Antonia's bedroom it seemed as sensible a place as any to begin the search.

She ran her hand through the layers of satin and crêpe de Chine and felt sick with envy as she thought of her day running up her parachute-silk undies.

No bottles, phials or pill-boxes. Antonia kept plenty in there to make a man's heart race, but nothing to make it stop.

The second drawer was deeper and had something more promising pushed to the back behind a nightdress—an antique rosewood box with mother-of-pearl inlay. Rose lifted it out. By the size and weight it probably contained letters or photographs. Frustratingly it was locked and there was no sign of a key. She cleared a space for it on top of the dressing table, opened the next drawer and almost at once found a tin containing curlers, safety-pins and other odds and ends including hairgrips. The lock on the box looked a simple fastening, so she tried poking the end of a hairgrip upwards through the keyhole. After a few attempts something clicked inside.

She opened the box.

On top was a photo of Vic, the lover, in cap and gown at some university ceremony. There were several old letters postmarked in the war years. A picture of an air-crew beside a Blenheim bomber. Printed dance invitations, pressed flowers, some twenty-first birthday cards. The sort of collection most women keep somewhere. No phials of poison. No letter from Manchester. She clicked her tongue impatiently. She was about to close the box when she noticed that the padded underside of the lid was hinged and had a small hook and hasp where it could unfasten. She eased it open. Out fell a folded document.

She'd seen it before. It was the death certificate Antonia had stolen from the Registry Office. The certificate intended for Hector. Nothing had yet been written on it. She held it a moment. The paper was shaking in her hand. Her impulse was to rip it to pieces, yet she hesitated.

Tear it up, the inner voice prompted her. And another immediately countered: don't —unless you want Antonia to know that you came up here and went through her things.

She folded the certificate and replaced it where she had found it and fiddled with the lock until it clicked back into place. She replaced the box in the drawer and told herself she was there to look for other things.

Where else?

She decided to try the top shelf in each of the wardrobes. They were too high for a proper inspection, so she carried across the stool from the dressing table and stood on it. She reached in among a collection of belts and hats.

And froze.

A sound had come from downstairs. She

was certain it was the front door being opened.

She held her breath and listened.

The front door clicked shut, beyond any question. She strained to hear. It was doubtful whether someone's tread on the hall carpet would carry up to her. A pulse was beating so loudly in her head that she could easily have taken it for footsteps.

Seconds passed. She let out a tremulous breath, like a swimmer just out of the water, and drew in more air.

A board gave a sharp creak. Then another. Whoever had entered the house was coming upstairs.

It can only be Hector, Rose told herself to stave off panic. Who else could have let themselves in? He must have come back from work to fetch something. He's going to that room on the first floor that he uses as his office. He won't have any reason to come up here.

The steps were perfectly audible now. They reached the turn after the first flight and continued upwards to the first floor. They didn't after all enter Hector's office. They continued up the next flight.

He was coming up to the bedroom.

She had to overcome the paralysis she felt

in her limbs. She couldn't be found delving into Antonia's wardrobe. She twisted her head to right and left, looking for somewhere to hide. Common sense told her she'd make a noise disturbing the hangers if she tried climbing in with the clothes. Better, surely, to accept that she'd be found in the room and think up some plausible reason for being there. But she didn't want to be caught standing on a stool with her arms in the wardrobe. She gripped the front of the shelf with both hands and made a stronger effort to use her legs. She staggered off the stool.

The footsteps reached the top stair and crossed the landing at the moment she pulled the stool away and closed the wardrobe. She backed against the wall, mentally rehearsing. 'Hello, Hector. I thought I heard you coming up. I happened to be passing so I brought a few groceries in and then I heard this noise upstairs so I came up to investigate. I'd quite forgotten about the cat being in the house. Am I very brave or very silly? Can I get you a cup of tea or anything?'

She heard him enter the bedroom and cross the room. He appeared to go towards one of the beds because there was a chink as if he'd picked up a piece of china or something on the bedside table and put it back. There followed the softer sound of the sheet on the bed being drawn back. Why was he touching the bedclothes? Surely he wasn't going to bed! Perhaps he had come home feeling ill. In that case, she'd have to wait for him to fall asleep. There was no way out except through the bedroom.

He didn't climb into the bed. He moved around the side of it and approached the open door of the dressing room.

Rose waited, flat to the wall, biting her underlip. He'd need to come right in to see her.

She saw the reflection first. It appeared in one of the side mirrors of the dressing table. And it wasn't Hector she saw.

21

It was Vic, Antonia's lover.

Immediately after Rose glimpsed him he turned away without appearing to notice her reflection, deciding, it seemed, that he had no reason to enter the dressing room. She didn't argue with that. She didn't move or breathe.

He prowled about the bedroom for a few seconds more. Then she heard him move out and start downstairs as if he was in no sort of hurry.

Her thoughts darted ahead of him. She'd hung her hat and coat on the hook behind the kitchen door. He would know for certain she was somewhere in the house if he looked in there. Never mind the coat; her handbag was on the kitchen table with some of the shopping.

She counted the flights of stairs, waiting for that loose board to shift under his weight and tell her that he was within a few steps of the ground floor. Half a lifetime seemed to pass before the rasp of wood travelled up to her.

She crept out to the corridor to listen over the stairwell. A door was opened down there. She clenched her right hand and put it to her mouth, for he had started talking to someone. The resonance of the voice reached her, but not the words. She strained to listen, and by degrees she decided that it was only one voice. He must have gone into the front drawing room and picked up the telephone, because when the talking stopped she heard the ping of the receiver being replaced.

She backed away from the banisters. She couldn't stand this much longer. If he came upstairs again she was certain she would scream.

Then she heard the front door being opened and shut.

When she was absolutely certain she was listening to the clatter of his steps in the street she ran back into the dressing room and moved as close to the window as she dared. The figure fast disappearing around the curve of the Crescent was unmistakably Vic.

Rose shook. She'd come all through the war without giving way to nerves. She'd always said in the air raids that it was up to each individual to control herself and stay calm. What a sanctimonious prig she'd been! She'd once watched a woman— a WAAF—run screaming from a shelter before the all-clear. Others had immediately started to cry hysterically. Pandemonium had broken out. The incident had infuriated Rose. She had felt that the woman deserved to be charged with cowardice or indiscipline or whatever King's Regulations called it. Now she herself knew what fear felt like. The urge to quit the house was overwhelming.

She should have taken a grip on herself and resumed the search she'd started. Instead she went downstairs and collected her things and left.

She walked fast down Portland Place towards Oxford Circus, wanting to shake off the physical and mental tensions. Keep moving, she told herself, and try to make sense of what happened. What was Vic doing there? He must have been in possession of a key to let himself in. His own key? Fat chance! The lover with a latchkey was an arrangement as likely to appeal to Antonia as darning socks.

No, Rose thought, Vic had been given the key for a different purpose—to check what had happened in the house in Antonia's absence. He had been sent to see if Hector's corpse was lying there. And he had phoned Antonia to report that it was not.

How foolhardy, how idiotic—to turn to Vic for help and put everything at risk!

Don't get angry, she told herself. Stay in control. How will Antonia react? She might convince herself that the poison was slow to take effect. She might think it was diluted in the curry and that a second helping will do the trick. She might even guess correctly that he didn't have any at all. After all the trouble she's taken over this plan she'll surely give it another night to work.

Rose carried on past Broadcasting House and All Souls into Upper Regent Street. Her step was still rapid, yet with more purpose in it than panic. She needed no proof of poisoning now, no more convincing that Hector's life was in her hands. It was almost noon and she had plenty to do.

She made her way across Oxford Circus to the top end of Regent Street. To Liberty's, to buy a nightdress. Thank God for that insurance money!

At the lingerie counter she asked to see the range. She was in luck. Some nightie and negligé sets in Swiss lawn had just come in. White, black and peach. The white looked marvellous against her skin. She pictured herself in the negligé, at home with Hector, in front of the bedroom fire, sipping champagne from the crystal glasses her glad-eyed Uncle Ben had given her as a wedding present. They'd never been used because Barry said champagne was for launching ocean liners. She would definitely find a shop that sold the stuff. And scent. The funds could run to something more alluring than the eau de Cologne she'd used for years.

'Will madam be taking the white?'

Madam took the white. And then took a taxi to Selfridges' to pick up a vintage

Pommery. After that to the cosmetics counter for a bottle of *Chypre* by Coty, some Arden powder, a cherry-coloured lipstick and a bottle of Cutex Cameo nail varnish.

After that it was laughable being driven back to Pimlico to open a tin of Spam for lunch. Rose promised herself that if she handled this evening smartly she wouldn't be living in her slum of a place much longer. She made a sandwich and some tea and ate standing up, taking drags at a cigarette between bites. Then she applied herself to getting the house into a state fit for a romantic encounter. She whisked round with a duster, throwing things into drawers. Upstairs she changed the sheets and pillowcases and laid the fires. Finally she threw some bath salts in the bath and ran the water. She allowed herself twenty minutes.

22

WHEN she left at half past three she was wearing the dreary green tweed overcoat that she meant to replace at the first opportunity, but under it the snazzy black and white dress she'd made for the Oldfield Gardens party on VE Day. And her new silk undies.

There was a worrying suggestion of fog in the afternoon air. She considered what to do if a real pea-souper came down. Hector might see it as a God-given excuse for her to stay the night in Park Crescent. If so, he was in for a disappointment. She'd feel like death in that great mausoleum of a bed-room surrounded by Antonia's things. And she wouldn't be any happier in a hotel room if he suggested it. That would be ghastly. She couldn't face it anywhere else but home.

She hailed a taxi in Vauxhall Bridge Road. The driver reckoned that in a couple of hours London would be at a standstill. Rose said she'd known fog to lift in a matter of minutes. He laughed.

'Lady, I won't argue with you, but don't ask me to come and fetch you. You're my last fare today.'

She didn't answer. She was thinking ahead. She would persuade Hector to drive her back to Pimlico, whatever the conditions.

She was sure it was no thicker by the time they pulled up outside Antonia's house. She paid the fare and took the key from her purse. She walked calmly up the steps and let herself in, resolved not to give way to the jitters. She was going to apply herself to the cooking.

She switched on the hall light.

'There you are, my flower!'

The voice hit her like a snapped violin string. Antonia was standing halfway up the stairs leaning languidly on the banisters as if she had been home all day. She was in a black sweater and slacks, manifestly relishing this moment.

Rose stared, speechless, her brain whirling.

'I see you left some shopping on the kitchen table, darling. Was that for Hector? I must settle up. I say, you look absolutely shattered. Is anything the matter?'

The words penetrated faintly to Rose's brain, as if she were buried under rubble. She wasn't listening anyway. She was thinking about her white nightie from Liberty's draped across the bed at home. And the champagne waiting in the sideboard.

She made an effort to say something intelligible. 'When did you get back?'

'Half an hour ago, no more. A little bird told me it was safe to come back, so I did.'

'Safe?'

'Hector.'

'What about Hector?'

'Darling, you did brilliantly.'

Her heart thumped. 'Did what, Antonia?'

'Rosie, dear, you don't have to put on an act for me. You know he's lying dead in the bathroom.'

She felt the blood drain from her face. She would faint any minute. She fought against it, letting her handbag drop and propping herself against the wall. 'He can't be. I don't believe you.'

Antonia was cruelly casual. 'I suppose something didn't agree with him. Could it have been your curry by any chance?'

'He didn't have any.'

'What?'

'I threw it away. We went to Reggiori's.'

Antonia stared at her for perhaps five seconds. 'For a quiet one, you're a fast worker.'

'Hector insisted on taking me.' Rose heard her voice thicken with anger. 'He ate none of that stuff you left in the fridge.'

The green eyes flashed. 'Why not, for God's sake? You really thought you had a chance, didn't you? Who the hell do you think you are, sneaking off to a restaurant with my husband? I gave you instructions. I went to the trouble of writing them down.'

'I don't believe he's dead.'

Antonia made a sound that was something between laughter and scorn. 'Come up and see, then. We've got to move him to the bedroom.'

'Then you killed him yourself.'

The voice took on a harder note, reinforced by a wagging finger. 'Watch what you say, darling. We're in this together. Sisters in crime. Remember? You'd better.'

'I've done nothing wrong.'

'Try telling that to the police.'

'You've called the police?'

'Idiot. They'll be onto us if we don't do something about the body. It's got to be carried up to the bedroom to look more natural when the undertaker comes. In case you've forgotten, I happen to possess a blank death certificate.'

Rose wetted her lips and tried to summon some inner strength. She didn't see how it was possible for Hector to be lying dead up there, but she had to find out. She stretched out her hand to the banister rail and started up the stairs. It felt like climbing out of a tar-pit.

'That's more like it, *chérie*.'

Antonia went ahead. She reached the top of the first flight and stepped to the room at the end talking like a ward sister dealing

224

with a student nurse. 'This is no picnic, I grant you, but it could be worse. We'll manage easily between us.'

When Rose reached the bathroom, Antonia was already inside, talking. 'It must have been quick. He couldn't have suffered much.'

The link in Rose's mind with hospital was reinforced by a pungent smell she distantly remembered from years ago, when she'd had her tonsils removed. She took a step into the bathroom and looked around the door. There was no corpse in there.

She jerked towards Antonia to protest and several things happened quickly. At the edge of her vision she caught a glimpse of something white flying towards her face. Her neck was seized from behind. She flung up her arm defensively and knocked the white object upwards. It reeked of the smell she'd noticed. She was being chloroformed.

Her neck was clamped in the crook of Antonia's arm. She was forced to gasp for air just as the pad was thrust towards her face again. This time she couldn't push it away. She succeeded in deflecting it slightly and turning her face aside. It missed her mouth and nostrils and made stinging contact with her cheek. She dragged it off with both hands and fought for possession of it.

She wasn't as strong as Antonia, but with her two hands she prised some of the fingers away.

Antonia removed the arm that was around Rose's neck and made a grab for the pad. She wasn't quick enough. Rose seized it from her and flung it into the bath. Momentarily Rose had the advantage. Antonia had reached out like a tennis player retrieving a serve and she only needed a push to lose her balance.

Rose supplied it.

Antonia crashed between the side of the bath and the wash basin, bringing down a glass shelf. If she was hurt it wasn't apparent. She recouped immediately.

Rose had turned to escape, but she was grabbed by the ankle and fell on her hands and knees. She was hauled in like a hooked fish. She kicked out with the free leg and caught some part of Antonia, possibly her chest.

There was a yelp of pain.

Rose's left ankle was given a vicious twist that forced her to roll on her back. At once Antonia hurled herself forward. She was unquestionably the stronger of them. Rose squirmed against the side of the bath to avoid being pinned down. They wrestled head to head. Then her hair was grabbed and her

226

head forced against the floor. Antonia pressed down on her, tugging viciously at her hair while she manoeuvred herself into a sitting position by bringing her knees up to the level of Rose's shoulders and forcing them down. Her thighs flattened Rose's breasts.

Rose looked up into the wildcat eyes. She felt a hand at her throat, forcing the collar apart and she believed she was going to be strangled. But the pressure came on the back of her neck. Her pearl necklace bit into her flesh and snapped as Antonia jerked it from her throat, scattering beads across the room.

'Cheap imitations, ducky.'

The face came closer. The blonde hair brushed Rose's cheek.

'What's that scent you're wearing? It stinks.' Antonia slapped her hard across the face.

She stared back and bore the pain in silence. Then she was conscious of a shift in the weight. Antonia was reaching behind her into the bath, groping for the pad of chloroform. Rose sensed an opportunity. Although her head was held and her shoulders were flat to the floor, her hips were still slightly angled against the bath. She flexed, raised her knees and got enough leverage from her feet to buck forward. Some hair was torn from her scalp in the process, but she managed to tip Antonia off completely and drag herself free.

She got off her knees, stepped clear of Antonia's flailing arms, and rushed out of the bathroom and along the corridor. She'd lost her shoes, which was an advantage in taking the stairs at speed. Antonia was up and in pursuit, but Rose was quicker. She jumped the last few steps and dashed across the hall to the door and dragged it open. The inrush of foggy air gave her hope. She lurched into the street and ran blindly.

23

A policeman in braces and with his sleeves rolled up opened the door of the room where Rose had been sitting for longer than she could estimate, bent forward with her face in her hands. He stood just inside, taking stock.

'Ready to talk now?'

She raised her head. She had panicked when they had brought her in and now despair had set in. She felt too exhausted to protest. Her brain rebelled at concocting a story that would satisfy them. She was certain she would get confused and blurt out the whole devastating truth.

'What time is it?'

'Just gone six.'

'Six in the morning?'

'You *are* in a state.'

'I'm thirsty.'

He went out, leaving the door open. Although she wasn't being kept in a cell, she was resigned to being transferred to one shortly. She had been driven here in a Black Maria with barred windows. This was just a place where they questioned people, somebody's office, with a desk and several chairs and hooks on the wall for coats. She'd kept hers on. The coke stove in the corner wasn't giving off much heat.

She had got off to a bad start with the desk sergeant by refusing to answer his questions. It was the first time she'd ever been in a police station. She hadn't trusted herself to say anything that wouldn't get her into trouble. Her silence had made the sergeant hostile. She was convinced that whatever she said he would keep her in custody. Up to now they didn't know anything about her except her name and where they had found her, but they'd break her down. It wouldn't take much.

A man she hadn't seen before brought in some tea in a chipped enamel mug. He had his jacket on, with a sergeant's stripes. He was silver-haired and his smile didn't sit well with his toothbrush moustache and drooping eyelids. He tried to pitch his voice to sound reasonable. And failed.

'So your name is Bell.'

'Yes.'

'Christian name?'

'Rose. I told the other man.'

'Mrs Rose Bell.' He'd noticed her ring, of course. 'Living with your husband?'

She didn't like the tone he used. It stung her into a response. 'He's dead.'

'The war?'

'No. Last month.'

'As recently as that?'

'It was an accident.' She stopped. She needn't have come out with this. She'd meant to say the minimum. Her nerves had betrayed her.

'Bad luck.' He didn't sound sympathetic. 'A road accident?'

No use denying it now. 'The tube. He fell off the platform.'

'Nasty. Not uncommon, though. Do you have any other family? Children?'

'No.'

230

'Have you got a permanent address, Mrs Bell?'

'Yes.'

He waited a moment. His voice slipped into a harder register. 'Come on, now. Let's have it. You're wasting police time.'

'In Pimlico. Oldfield Gardens.'

'Pimlico. Yet one of our patrols found you on Paddington Station in the small hours of the morning. Is that where you normally spend the night? It's a long way from Pimlico. I'd have thought Victoria Station was more convenient.'

He kept looking at her legs. The ruins of her stockings hung in ribbons.

He developed his theme. 'It all depends what you were up to, doesn't it? I'm told by certain ladies who parade there that Paddington is better for business than any other London terminus.' Seeing the outrage in her eyes, he smiled. 'But they don't take kindly to newcomers, as you appear to have discovered. What happened to your shoes?'

She was bitterly insulted. 'That's a filthy suggestion! I demand an immediate apology.'

'Do you now? What are you wearing under that coat, then? It looks pretty tarty to me.'

'Bloody hell!' Her anger galvanized her.

She was damned if she'd give in to personal abuse. She'd grown up in awe of policemen. They were fatherly figures who helped you across the road and told you the time if you asked, but she would cut this bastard down to size because she didn't see a decent London bobby standing in front of her; she saw a reincarnation of Barry, a sneering, sarcastic bully, who despised and resented women. She wasn't putting up with any more of it.

'Fetch your superior, please.'

The grin vanished. 'Hold on, Mrs Bell. There's no need for that.'

'I want to make an official complaint.'

'All right. I spoke out of turn. I withdraw everything I just said.'

She glared at him. 'You were asking about my shoes. I lost them on the train.' The lie came readily to her lips. She would lie and lie to this sadist.

He asked which train.

'The tube.'

'So you took the tube?'

'Yes.'

'You bought a ticket, I hope.'

'Of course I did.'

'Where would that have been? Victoria?'

She nodded.

'Right, then.' He folded his arms aggressively. He was looking for an opening and when he found it he would be ruthless. 'Just tell me how you were able to pay for the ticket without possessing a handbag or even a purse?'

'I lost my bag on the train.'

'Along with the shoes, I suppose. London Transport Lost property Office is having a busy night. I presume you had your Identity Card in the handbag?'

'Yes—and it might be a damned sight more useful if instead of persecuting me you got on with the job you're paid to do and found my things for me.' With that, she put her hands over her face and sobbed loudly. See how he coped with that, the swine.

He tried without much success to sound like an uncle. 'Well, my dear, I've got to get the facts to know the rights and wrongs of it, haven't I? Where were you going on the tube?'

She sniffed. 'Nowhere in particular.' She had a good thought. 'I was on the Circle Line. I was depressed. I couldn't stand it at home when I thought of what had happened to . . . .'

'Your husband?'

'Yes.' Another sob. 'So I went down the

tube, meaning to—oh, I don't know what I meant to do, I was in such a state.' The lies were coming fluently. She'd needed that stinging reminder of her late husband. Barry had got no more than he deserved. But the police wouldn't see it that way. She was fighting to get out of this place.

'And you got off at Paddington?' His probing was more conciliatory.

'Great Portland Street.' Her brain was working better. From the state of her feet it was obvious that she'd done some walking. 'I got off at Great Portland Street and walked to Paddington.'

'Did you have any reason to make for Paddington?'

'No particular reason. I just kept walking in the fog.' Rose gave a little-girl-lost look. She decided to consolidate. 'Could I have some tea, please?' She put her hand to her head. 'And some aspirin?'

He ignored the plea. 'You didn't get those scratches on your neck by walking.'

She'd been aware of some discomfort, but then her entire body was aching. She found the scratches and traced them with her fingers.

'They're fresh. And what happened to your cheek? It's bright red.'

234

The place where the chloroform had made contact. 'I must have walked into something.'

'A right-hander, by the look of it. There's no two ways about it—you were in a fight, and you didn't come off best. Look at your coat.'

'I was attacked in the tube. They stole my bag.'

'And your shoes?'

'To stop me giving chase.'

'This is more like it. Description?'

She shook her head. 'I fainted. I don't remember.'

'Then how do you know you were in a fight?'

'You just told me.'

The sides of his mouth turned down and he marched out and slammed the door.

Presently a constable came in with a tray. When Rose saw the aspirin and the two biscuits, elation flooded into her weary body. She knew she was winning.

In about twenty minutes the sergeant returned. 'Your husband was Wing Commander Bell who was killed on Knightsbridge Underground Station on October 10th?'

'Yes.'

'I want you to give the constable a description of the things you lost, the bag and the shoes. Then we're sending you home. I suggest you see your doctor next time you feel depressed. It's better than travelling the Circle Line.'

24

SHE was led out to a police car and seated in the rear next to a young officer with a Welsh accent who offered her a cigarette and struck a match for her.

'Pimlico, is it, Mrs Bell?'

'Oldfield Gardens. Have they finished with me, then?'

'You can relax now.'

Relax? she thought. Jesus Christ, the chance would be a fine thing! She drew on the cigarette and saw it shake in her fingers.

I was almost murdered last night. There's no question that Antonia tried to kill me. That was no pillow fight.

And it was no spur-of-the-moment attack. Antonia lured me up there, into a trap. She had the chloroform ready in the bathroom. Where could she have got hold of chloroform?

Vic! He works in a science lab. She and Vic are in this together.

Two's company, three's a crowd.

When I met Antonia, she didn't tell me about Vic. I stupidly believed the desperate things we agreed to do were a secret between two women. A pact. Now I know Antonia has a stronger loyalty.

Antonia and Vic have decided to eliminate me. They think I doublecrossed them because I failed to poison Hector.

If they killed me, how would they hope to get away with it? It's ghastly to think about, but how would they dispose of my body? They need the blank death certificate for Hector. Presumably they'd bury me in some deserted place.

'Oldfield Gardens, is it, Mrs Bell?'

'What?'

'Where you live.'

'Oh, yes.'

'Feeling shaken up, are you?'

'Just a little. I lost my key. How am I going to get in?'

'We'll force the lock, unless you keep a spare under the mat.'

'No.'

'Pity. Sensible, though.'

They turned into her street.

'It's the last one on the left.'

She stepped out of the car forgetting that

she was still without shoes and gasped as her feet touched the pavement. The driver supported her arm and helped her through the gate.

'Don't worry, Mrs Bell. We'll have you indoors in no time. PC Owen has a rare knack of getting through locked doors, haven't you, Taff?'

Constable Owen rounded the front of the car. 'We won't need to. There's someone inside.'

Rose had started to say that such a thing was impossible when the front door swung open and Antonia looked out.

The devil.

'Rose, darling, what on earth has happened to you? Was there an accident?'

Rose went rigid.

The constable responded by bringing his hand more firmly around her arm. 'Right, Mrs Bell. Got to get you inside.'

Antonia, her features creased in concern, stepped forward and came along the path. 'She's been missing all night. She doesn't know what she's doing or saying half the time. It's the shock. Has she told you? The poor little soul lost her husband last month. Come on, my flower, you'll freeze out here.

I've got a lovely fire going in the front room.' She reached out to take Rose's other arm.

'No!'

'It's tragic, officer. I don't know what she's been telling you, but I've known her for years. Isn't that right, Rose? I won't say how much I've done to help her these last weeks. That's the way friends should be. We stick together like sisters.' She looked into Rose's eyes. 'I mean it goes without saying, doesn't it?'

Rose knew with numbing certainty what she meant. Never mind what went without saying. She'd said it. They stuck together. Sisters in crime.

She turned to the constable. 'I want to get back in the car.'

Antonia smiled knowingly at the police and cast her eyes upwards.

The grip on Rose's arm tightened. 'Sorry, my love, but no can do. We're on patrol. We need that seat for real villains. In you go. You'll get pneumonia out here.'

He didn't address her as Mrs Bell. That patronizing 'my love' told her that they'd swallowed everything Antonia had said. Blitzed by fear, anger and the cold, she allowed them to steer her into the house. She was through.

Constable Owen was talking to Antonia. 'She lost her handbag and shoes in the tube. We've got a description. I suggest she tries London Transport Lost property Office just in case.'

Rose felt like a hospital patient being discussed by the staff. She sank into an armchair in the front room beside the fire she'd laid for her romantic evening with Hector. The coal was well alight. She shut her eyes, shut out the world.

Antonia took charge. 'Who's good at making tea? I'd better do something about this poor lamb's feet.'

She was too overpowering for the police. They made excuses and left so fast that Rose heard the front door close and the car being started before her bemused brain grasped that she was alone with the woman who'd tried to murder her.

'Get those stockings off.'

She opened her eyes.

Antonia was standing over her with a bowl in her hands like an angel of mercy. Her voice slipped into a more mellow tone. '. . . or what's left of them. You want to clean up your feet, don't you?' She set the bowl on the floor. 'I had to use the kettle. The boiler's out.'

Bemused and obedient, Rose felt under her skirt and unfastened the tattered stockings and peeled them off. The contact with the warm water was heaven.

'Soap?'

Under the cool inspection of the green eyes, she worked on her feet. The soles were sore and the skin was broken in several places. They felt better for being clean and warm.

She looked up. 'I can't fight any more. Let's get it over with.'

'Mm?' Now Antonia seemed bemused.

'Finishing what you started yesterday evening. Killing me.

'Killing you, darling? You *are* confused. Why on earth should I want to do that? Oh, I don't deny that I tried to put you to sleep for a few minutes, and I'm sorry it turned into the tussle it did. You certainly pack a punch.'

'Antonia, I'm not that stupid. You came at me like a tigress after blood.'

'Of course. I was so flaming mad that I lashed out and lost control.' She laughed. 'You know me.'

'You're lying. It was planned. You had a pad of chloroform.'

Antonia was ready to justify anything.

241

'Sweetie, I trusted you and you let me down. Instead of cooking that meal for Hector you threw it away and went to Reggiori's.'

'I was afraid I'd poison him.'

'Obviously.'

'Well, I knew you wanted to get rid of him. I couldn't knowingly poison anybody. That's hideously cruel.'

'You knew damn all. I didn't say anything about poison.'

'You didn't need to say anything. It was obvious.'

'What you're telling me, Rose darling, is that you felt sorry for the poor beggar. Let's put our cards on the table. You developed quite a pash for my old man. I saw the warpaint and the glad rags last night. I never had a cook who wore pearls and French perfume. Is it any wonder I lashed out? Don't get me wrong. It wasn't that I was jealous. It was the deceit. You and I had an understanding.'

'And for that you'd murder me?'

'Not you, darling.'

'For God's sake, Antonia! You tried to chloroform me.'

'Only to put you out for a bit. I couldn't trust you any more, could I? I just meant to give you a whiff and get you out of my hair while I attended to Hector.'

Rose pressed her lips together and glared back, too angry to speak, refusing to be soft-soaped.

'In the event,' Antonia continued in the same breezy manner, 'you ran off into the fog, which saved me some trouble. When Hector came in I was ready for him. And now I need your help with some lifting.'

Rose stared at her.

'The corpse, darling. It's lying in the hall at home. We've got to move it upstairs to the bedroom before we fetch the under-taker. It's got to look as if he died in bed. The face is slightly marked like yours. Not enough to cause comment, fortunately.'

Every muscle tightened. 'This isn't true. You're a liar.'

Antonia sighed. 'I can't deny that, kit-ten. I did mislead you yesterday. Didn't want you getting in the way. This time Hec-tor really is dead. I slapped the chloroform over his face the minute he stepped through the front door yesterday evening. Put him to sleep and then smothered him with a cush-ion.' She picked her handbag off a chair and unfastened it. 'Look, I've filled in his name on the death registration certificate. And the date.'

Rose saw the name boldly inked in. A few words written on paper proved nothing and she wanted to say so but her throat had tightened too much for speech. The description of Hector's death in that entrance hall in Park Crescent was horribly credible. Suddenly she wanted Antonia to be lying, desperately wanted her to have invented this grotesque admission of murder, even though it meant another deathtrap had been set for herself. She couldn't cope with the thought of Hector dead.

She'd thought she was beyond the point where anything could hurt her. This extinguished the last hope of any future. She handed back the paper.

Antonia took her silence as satisfaction. 'Get something on your feet and we'll go now. I'll get you some breakfast there. There's nothing here.'

Rose stayed seated. She had just come to her senses. There was a flaw in what was being suggested. 'You don't need my help. You've got Vic to assist you. If there really was a body he could lift it.'

'Vic?' From the pitch of the voice it might have been the Archbishop of Canterbury.

'Vic doesn't know Hector is dead. God, we don't want Vic to find out.'

'Stop playing the innocent, Antonia. He's your lover. I know you've told him everything because I was there in your house yesterday morning when you sent him to check whether Hector was poisoned. Do you understand? I was there. I came early. He didn't see me, but I saw him. He went up to the bedroom and looked inside. And then he went downstairs and used the telephone and I'm certain he was phoning you.'

She treated it casually, walking out of the room and into the kitchen as she spoke. 'You're right about one thing, Rosie dear, he did phone me. Weren't you near enough to listen? Pity. Listen, how can I get it into your head that there wasn't any poison in the damned curry? That meat was perfectly edible and so was everything else.'

Rose dug her fingers into the arms of the chair. 'In that case, why did you give Vic a key and send him to the house?'

'This is gospel truth,' the answer came back from the kitchen. 'He wasn't looking for a corpse. He was trying to find out whether you'd spent the night with Hec.'

Rose frowned.

Antonia came back with a towel that

she was twisting between her hands. 'Yes, I sent him round, Rosie. I've been staying with him in Knightsbridge instead of visiting my wretched old Mum in Manchester, as if you hadn't guessed.'

'How much does he know?'

'Vic? Sweet F.A., darling. He thinks all this was a love trap for you and my sneaky little husband, and I must say, I had suspicions of my own when I learned from Hector's own lips that he'd taken you out to dinner.' She let that sink in. 'I'd better confess that it wasn't the total surprise to me that I registered yesterday. That was a little mischief on my part. I wanted to hear it from your own angelic lips. Actually I'd already talked to Hec on the telephone yesterday morning, playing the doting wife, enquiring whether you'd made him a decent curry. He was positively chirpy when he told me he'd taken you to Reggiori's instead. Apart from being bloody annoyed I was curious to know what it amounted to. After all, if you two had given me evidence of adultery I could have divorced him. No need for a funeral. Unluckily for Hector, Vic couldn't find a single brown hair on the pillows.' She let the towel unfurl and tossed it to Rose.

'Pity. You could have saved me no end of bother.'

25

ANTONIA had left the Bentley round the corner in Charlwood Street. She didn't speak until they were travelling in slow convoy up Vauxhall Bridge Road with the early morning traffic from south of the river.

'Rose.'

'Yes?'

'Why are you doing this?'

'Doing what?'

'Coming back to the house with me. It's only for Hector's sake, isn't it?'

'Does it matter?' Rose stared ahead at the adverts on the back of a bus. She felt weary, but more in control. Before leaving the house she had fitted in a wash and forced herself to eat a slice of bread and Marmite. She was wearing stockings and shoes again and a jumper and skirt. She had also dug out her grey demob overcoat that buttoned at the neck.

Antonia persisted with her point about Hector. 'The fact is, you want to find out for yourself if he's really dead. You don't know whether to believe me.'

'Can you blame me?'

Antonia smirked. 'He cared bugger all about you. You know that, don't you? Women were always making fools of themselves over bloody Hector, wanting to mother him.'

'Who said I wanted to mother him?'

She gave a single, high-pitched laugh. 'If it was sex you wanted, he just wasn't up to it, sweetie, believe me.'

'It takes two.'

'Go to hell,' Antonia snapped back, no longer amused. 'That's bloody good coming from you. It takes two! How was it with Barry, then? Did you satisfy him? You and who else? Was it two or two hundred?'

Rose didn't answer. Her other compelling reason for agreeing to come was that she needed to keep tabs on this murderous woman after two nasty shocks in twenty-four hours. She meant to stick with her now until it was safe to be alone again.

Antonia steered the car through the mews entrance behind Park Crescent and into a garage.

'Come on, then. Come and see for yourself.'

She opened a gate and let them into the yard at the back of the house where the two dustbins stood. Then she unlocked the kitchen door and led the way in. Yesterday's shopping still lay unused on the table.

Rose followed, her skin suddenly so sensitive that she was acutely conscious of every movement of her clothes. Pulses throbbed in her face and neck. She said a silent, desperate prayer that Hector might still be alive.

Antonia crossed the room and hesitated at the door that led to the hall. Rose tensed, sensing that she ought to be ready to defend herself against another sudden attack. Then Antonia spoke over her shoulder. 'Take a long, deep breath, my poppet.'

They stepped into the hall.

Rose took the breath, and held it. And held it longer.

Just inside the front door, where Antonia had said it would be, lay a corpse in a camel-hair overcoat like the one Hector had worn to Reggiori's. Dark trousers and brown shoes. Hands still in leather gloves. An ear partly covered by a black woollen scarf. Curly red-gold hair.

'Want to look at the face?' Antonia was standing beside the body preparing to give the shoulder a prod with her foot.

'There's no need.' Rose heard herself say in a flat voice that sounded like someone reading lines without understanding them. She picked up a green porkpie hat that was lying against the skirting board. 'It can't be anyone else.'

Outwardly controlled, she ached from her throat to the pit of her stomach. It wasn't the piercing pain of shock; she had felt increasingly certain from the way Antonia had been behaving that this time she had spoken the truth. No, it was grief that she felt, a bitter, grinding grief for Hector and for the loss of a life that she had known was threatened and she would have saved.

'Feeling strong?' Antonia took off her coat and threw it over a chair. 'Do you need a snifter first or shall we get started?'

'Do you want to move him?'

'I didn't bring you here for tea and biscuits.'

'All right. Let's do it now.' Rose steeled herself. Numb as she felt, she was determined not to give way to panic in front of Antonia. She placed Hector's hat respectfully on a chair and stepped closer.

She wasn't new to the sight of death. She had seen air-raid victims brought out on stretchers from bombed buildings and she

250

had gone through the ordeal of identifying Barry at the mortuary. But this was the first time she had been called upon to touch a corpse.

'You take the legs, then. We'd better get him straight first.'

The body was lying on its side in a bowed attitude with the left leg bent into a near right angle and the other almost straight. His left arm lay along the length of the body and the right was trapped under the head.

It was necessary to bring the legs together to lift them. She moistened her lips and told herself to treat it straightforwardly as a simple, mechanical task. To forget that this had been Hector. Stooping, she took hold of the bent leg above the ankle. She gave a gasp of shock and let go at once. Through the trousers it felt as if the limb were encased in plaster.

Antonia had taken hold of the arm that lay under the head and was trying unsuccessfully to straighten it. 'God, he's as stiff as a board.'

'Is it rigor mortis?'

'It must be.'

'I think I do need that drink.'

'You're not the only one.'

They moved into one of the sitting rooms

and Antonia poured generous brandies into wine glasses. She spilled some and didn't even notice. She had gone very pale.

Rose made an effort to be practical. 'It wears off after a time, I believe.'

'Any idea how long?'

'No.'

'There's no movement at all. It'll be the devil to get upstairs. It's the arms and legs. They're in such awkward positions.'

'Can we wait for it to wear off?'

'And leave him lying in the hall? It could be hours and hours. It only wants someone to knock at the door and we're sunk. Christ Almighty, Rose, why didn't I think of this?'

Rose was incapable of dealing with anyone else's state of panic, least of all Antonia's. The revulsion she'd felt when she handled that hardened limb had taken a grip on her mind.

Antonia stood in the middle of the room with hunched shoulders and folded arms. 'Even if we managed to get him up to the bedroom how would I get him into pyjamas? I'd have to rip them apart to get the arms and legs in. Blast you, Hector!'

'Is it important to have him in pyjamas?'

'*Important?* He's supposed to have died in

bed, of cardiac failure. I've written it on the death certificate.'

To Rose there seemed only one feasible course of action, but she wasn't going to suggest it herself. She waited for it to come from Antonia, as it eventually did.

'We'll have to drag him into one of these rooms for the time being and move him later.'

'I don't think I can bear to touch him again.'

'Bloody hell.'

She despised herself for giving way after she had held herself together so well. 'You can say it. I'm a coward.'

Antonia curled her lip and said rather more. 'If you fill your knickers over a little thing like this, I don't like to think about your date with Mr Pierrepoint.'

'Who's that?'

'The hangman.'

It was a telling threat. Rose had a vivid mental picture of herself in the execution chamber. Even in the black hours after Barry's death she had never let her thoughts move on so far as that horrid possibility. She stared at Antonia for some seconds. 'All right. I'll try.'

They went out into the hall again. Rose

253

took a grip of one of the coat sleeves. Shoulder to shoulder they dragged the body to the back room.

'On the sofa.'

'He won't look natural.'

'Shut up and pick up the legs.'

Rose obeyed. She avoided looking directly at the face and as soon as the job was done she ran to the toilet and retched repeatedly.

In the kitchen Antonia made black coffee. When she put the cup in front of Rose there were two pills beside it.

Rose turned them over suspiciously. 'What are these?'

'Benzedrine. I get them on prescription from my doctor. I'm supposed to be slimming. Try them.'

'Not likely.'

'What's up? It's going to be another long night. They'll keep you awake. Give you a marvellous feeling in your head. Didn't you take them in the war?'

Rose took a sip of the coffee and said nothing.

'Oh, for pity's sake!' Antonia snatched up the pills and swallowed them.

They sat without saying anything to each other. Soon the silence became unendurable. Antonia switched on the wireless. Someone was playing a cinema organ. Finally Antonia went out to see if the state of the body had altered. She shook her head when she came back.

'Just the same. I was planning to see the undertaker this morning.'

'You can't have him here yet.'

'I could ask him not to come until late.'

'How do we know when it wears off? It could be hours and hours. Haven't you got a medical book in the house?'

'I never bother with books.'

'You've got a room stacked with them upstairs.' Rose realized as she spoke that she hadn't mentioned going upstairs before. Antonia shot her a look.

Searching for information in some book was better than doing nothing. They went up and eventually found an *Enquire Within Upon Everything* that omitted to mention rigor mortis. Most of the books were in foreign languages.

'Hector could have told us to the minute,' said Antonia with an oddly belated note of pride in her murdered husband. 'He was very well informed on things like that.'

Rose thought what stupid comments people come out with in times of stress.

26

SHORTLY after three that afternoon they
were admitted to the office of Longshot and
Greely, Funeral Directors, an oak-panelled
or more likely oak-veneered inner room behind a curtained shopfront in Marylebone
Road. When Rose was introduced as Antonia's friend and Mr Greely put out his
hand, she had to steel herself to make the
first human contact since handling Hector.
Her sense of touch was more sensitive than
ever she had suspected. Actually she would
have found Greely's soft handshake obnoxious at any time. Probably he was not much
over forty, but his movements were decrepit.

'Park Crescent? I know it like my own
house, ladies. That magnificent colonnade.
And such commodious houses. Rest assured
that any arrangements you should favour us
with will meet the highest standards. Longshot and Greely have conducted funerals for
some of the great families of London for

generations. We shall be honoured to perform this last duty for your dear father.'

'Husband.' Antonia corrected him from under a veil. She had changed into a black fitted coat with frogged fastenings.

'Indeed?' An additional set of furrows appeared on Greely's brow. 'My dear lady, forgive me. One assumed . . . . You appear so young for such a tragic eventuality.'

'It was his heart.'

'Ah.'

'There was a weakness. We'd known of it for years.'

'Even so.'

'Exactly.'

'Was it sudden when it came?'

'Completely. He died at home in the drawing room.'

'Today?'

'Yesterday, about six in the evening.'

'And he is still there? Have no worries, my dear lady. I shall arrange for him to be conveyed to our chapel of rest within the hour. From what you say I assume that there will be no need of an inquest and we can proceed with the arrangements within the next few days. I dare say you are too distressed to discuss such things as yet, but possibly tomorrow . . . .'

'I want to settle it now.' Antonia spoke in a soft, yet decisive voice.

'We shall see to it, provided, of course, that you find our terms satisfactory.'

Rose thought it appropriate to contribute something to the conversation since she was supposed to be the widow's support. 'It will be a very quiet occasion.'

'Cremation,' said Antonia.

'Whatever you wish, ladies. I take it that the deceased—your late husband—expressed a preference for cremation.'

'He wasn't opposed to it.'

'How soon can you arrange it?' asked Rose.

'Ladies, there will be no delay in my firm's arrangements, I assure you. However, the Cremation Regulations do require us to observe certain formalities. Paperwork. Very tedious.'

Antonia opened her bag. 'We brought the registrar's certificate.'

'Yes.' He held it folded in his hand. 'In point of fact, I must give *you* some forms to be completed.'

Antonia opened her bag and took out her fountain pen. 'We'll do it now.'

'I'm afraid not,' said Greely. 'Form A is a declaration that you must make in the presence of a Justice of the peace or a Commissioner for Oaths.'

'Is there one nearby? If it's only a matter of visiting an office, we'll do it this afternoon.'

'Ah, but as there has been no inquest, I must also let you have forms B and C, the medical certificate forms. Form B must be filled in by the doctor who certified the death and Form C is for another doctor of at least five years standing, who should also see the —em—body. Then all the forms, including this certificate you obtained from the registry have to be sent to the Medical Referee of the London Cremation Company for his written authority.'

There was a petrifying silence.

'I understand your feelings, ladies, believe me. I wish the procedure could be simplified. It is, of course, a safeguard against deaths that happen in suspicious circumstances —not that this remotely applies in your case.'

Rose glanced at Antonia's strained face and then back at Greely. 'What is the procedure for a burial?'

'Oh, much more straightforward.'

Antonia reached a rapid decision. 'We'll have him buried, then. I just can't face all these delays.'

Rose nodded. It was the obvious thing to do. They couldn't run the risk of forging the medical forms as well as the registration certificate. Burial was the answer. It wasn't as if Hector's body contained poison or had any obvious injuries. Even an exhumation wouldn't reveal anything.

Greely seemed encouraged by Antonia's change of mind. 'Then we *can* attend to things at once. Let's make sure that this registration is all in order. Forty-two, was he, poor fellow? No age at all. And I dare say you also have the other piece of paper in your bag?'

Antonia frowned and opened her handbag. 'No, what's that?'

'If you left it at home, it doesn't matter at this stage. Doesn't matter in the least as long as you bring it tomorrow.'

Rose tensed and crossed her legs. 'What is this piece of paper? She gave you the certificate.'

He opened a drawer in his desk and took out a form and held it up briefly for their scrutiny. 'It looks like this. This one re-lates to a burial last week. The registrar will have issued a similar one with your copy of the registration certificate. You see, I don't actually require the document you handed me. That is for your use. I require the other—' He coughed behind his hand. '—the disposal certificate, as it's known.'

'The what?' Antonia raised her voice in a manner hardly fitting a just-bereaved widow.

'It's the certificate that authorizes me as the funeral director—or whoever you should honour with the arrangements—to conduct the burial. Without it, I am unable to proceed.'

Antonia shot a horrified glance at Rose. 'I didn't bring it with me.'

Greely smiled reassuringly. 'Not to worry. Not to worry at all. It isn't the first time. people get confused, and understandably in the circumstances. Why don't you see if it's at home, and if it isn't, if you've mislaid it, I can apply to the registrar for a duplicate.'

'No, you will not.'

'Oh, there's no extra fee. I'll tell you what I suggest. You ladies go back to the house and see if this elusive little form is lying about somewhere. In the meantime I'll drive over with one of my colleagues to collect—that is to say, take care of—your late husband, and if for any reason the certificate is lost—'

'No.' Antonia cut him off in mid-sentence. She stood up and snatched the registration certificate from his desk. 'I've never been treated with such callous and pettifogging disregard. I came here looking for sympathy and understanding and you talk to me about *disposal*, as if my Hector is unwanted rubbish. After this I couldn't bear to put him in your hands. We'll get someone with a modicum of respect for the departed to do it. Come on, Rose, before I say something I regret.'

'Madam, I apologize most sincerely. I assure you I was merely trying to explain the formalities. Upsetting you like this is the very last thing I wanted.'

Rose wasted no sympathy on him either as she followed Antonia out. 'It's the last you'll hear from us, anyway.'

Out in the street Antonia stood tight-lipped beside the car. Although Rose felt in a state of panic too, she offered to drive. In the WAAF she'd driven everything from staff cars to two-ton lorries.

Antonia's voice was bleak. 'What on earth do we do now?'

'Better go somewhere quiet where we can think. Round the Park.'

Rose started up and swung the Bentley into Baker Street and across Park Road to join the traffic on the Outer Circle. For all she cared now, they could drive round and round Regent's park until the petrol ran out, a sort of limbo. Hell wasn't far away.

Eventually Antonia spoke in a flat, embittered voice. 'What did he call it?'

'A disposal certificate. God, what a laugh! After all our trouble he didn't need the death certificate at all.'

Antonia was white with shock. 'I'm devastated. Why did I walk out of there? Now that it's too bloody late I can see what we should have done. We should have let him collect the body. He wanted the job. He would have overlooked the wretched form. He could have stretched a point. He kept saying it wasn't important.'

'I don't think so, Antonia. Once he'd seen the body he'd quietly ask the registrar's office for one, and that would be curtains for you and me.'

'It's curtains anyway.'

They passed the Zoo entrance and Gloucester Gate before either spoke again. This time Antonia's anger switched to Rose. 'You knew about this all along, didn't you?'

'What?'

'The bloody disposal certificate. What else? You must have had one for Barry. So why didn't you tell me?'

'Dry up, Antonia! I didn't even look at the wretched forms. I just handed them over to the bank. They acted as executors, so they did everything. For God's sake get it out of your head that I tried to undermine the plan. We wouldn't be in this mess if I could have avoided it and that's the truth.'

The force of this reasoning evidently impressed Antonia, because she took a more positive line. 'Is there any way we can get hold of one of those damned forms?'

'Only from the registry office.'

'By reporting Hector's death, you mean? That's out. We'd have to get a doctor to look at the body first and write out a certificate.'

'Do you think a doctor could tell what happened?'

'He'd order a post mortem for sure. Perfectly healthy men don't drop dead without some reason.'

'Was Hector fit?'

'He never had a day off work that I can remember.'

'So he never saw a doctor. We could ask *any* doctor to look at him.'

'Duckie, even the most pea-brained, superannuated, gin-sodden GP in the world knows bloody well that sudden death has to be reported to the coroner.'

Rose wasted no more words. Her mind was made up. She spun the wheel and turned sharp left into Albany Street, raced through the gears and stamped on the accelerator.

'Christ! Where the heck are we going?'

'You'll see.'

27

As Rose reversed the car into a space in Lowndes Square she admitted that they wouldn't be working to a plan. In Air Force parlance it was chocks away and let us pray.

The entrance to the Stationery Office depot was manned by a burly ex-serviceman with two rows of ribbons and a seen-it-all-before look. He said nobody was ever allowed inside without an appointment and then stared over their heads as if that were the end of it. Rose kept talking. And when she told him she was Barry Bell's widow it worked like a password. He beamed and grasped her hand. Wing Commander Bell had been a particular pal of his with a wicked sense of humour just like his own and the depot could do with a few more like him.

It was a long time since Rose had found cause to be thankful to Barry.

She explained that she had been asked by Mr Gascoigne to collect some of her husband's things and since she was still not coping very well alone she had brought her friend.

The doorman wrote out a pass for them and ordered a messenger boy to take the two ladies to Gascoigne's office. They were led through swing doors and along a corridor painted in institutional green and cream. A second set of doors opened into a place of a size and scale they were unprepared for, a warehouse as long as the nave of St Paul's, with rank upon rank of metal storage racks where the pews would had been.

Rose's nerve faltered. She glanced Antonia's way and rolled her eyes upwards.

Antonia shook her head and gave the V-sign.

Gascoigne's office was higher than everything else, mounted on struts like a watchtower. They climbed an iron staircase, and had to be let into the office to wait because he wasn't inside. Through windows the length of each wall they could see brown-coated civil servants between the racks collecting packets of stationery and loading them on to hand-trolleys.

While the boy went to look for Gascoigne

the two women stared out at the scene. Antonia asked if Barry had been one of the trolley-pushers.

'He must have been.'

'Can't imagine it.'

Rose could, without difficulty. She wasn't a believer in the occult, yet she had a disturbing sense of his presence here. Listening to the doorman she had sharply visualized the wisecracking clever dick who was her husband striding through that entrance with some fresh quip to brighten the day. All along the corridor she had been conscious of him, into the warehouse and up the stairs and now if she turned her head he would be just behind her in one of those brown overalls, grinning all over his face at what had happened to her and what she was desperate enough to be planning now.

Bastard. She still hated him. Soon after they'd married he'd given up bothering to amuse *her*. All the bonhomie was directed at other people.

Antonia said someone was coming.

'Oh, God.'

'He's only a man, darling.'

Gascoigne had come up the stairs in a rush and was breathless. He was in the same dark grey pinstripe he'd worn at the funeral. He held out his hand. 'My dear Mrs Bell, they didn't tell me you were expected this afternoon.'

'They didn't know. We just happened to be passing. This is Mrs Ashton who is helping me attend to things.' Not entirely untruthful. Ashton had been Antonia's maiden name. And they were attending to things.

A small stack of chairs stood in one corner. Gascoigne lifted two out and dusted them with his handkerchief. 'How are you feeling now, Mrs Bell?'

'Not much better, I'm afraid.'

'It's early days.'

'You mentioned some articles of my husband's.'

'Yes, indeed.' He opened a desk and took out a brown envelope. 'Would you care to check them?'

'That's all right.'

He coughed. 'I meant would you be good enough to check them. Perhaps it's fussy of me, but I need a receipt.' He flapped his hand vaguely. 'Bureaucracy, I'm afraid.'

She let the things slide out on to his desk. A Swan fountain pen that she had seen Barry use at home to fill in his football coupon. Two tickets for a dance at the Hammersmith Palais on October 12th—one date loverboy had been unable to keep. Finally a snapshot. She got a jolt as if Barry himself had nudged her. The picture was of a woman holding a child, a boy of eighteen months or so. She turned it over. In a neat, small hand was written, 'To Darling B from Mike and Me'.

She tore it in two and dropped it into the wastepaper basket with the dance tickets and the envelope.

Gascoigne looked shocked. 'I seem to have dragged you here unnecessarily.'

Antonia beamed at him. 'Not at all. The pen will come in useful, if it's only to sign your receipt.' She picked it up and handed it to Rose, who scribbled her signature on the slip of paper Gascoigne had ready.

Gascoigne thanked her. 'Will you have a cup of tea? It's past the time, but I'm sure the ladies downstairs will rise to the occasion. Wing Commander Bell was very popular with them.'

'No doubt.' Rose was choking with bitterness from seeing the photograph. She pressed her hankie to her face and told herself angrily to stay in control. Then she stood up and glanced out of the window at the storage racks. 'What would really please me would be to see exactly where he worked.'

Gascoigne paled. 'That's not possible, I'm sorry to say.'

Antonia chipped in. 'Oh, I say, you can't mean that, Mr Gascoigne. You don't know what a comfort it would be.'

'It's a matter of security.'

'No, darling. Humanity. It's a matter of humanity. What do you think she's going to do—steal a ration book?'

'Goodness, no.'

'Well, then?' She moved closer to Rose and slipped her arms around her and looked appealingly at Gascoigne.

'There are regulations.'

'You're just obeying orders, is that it? That excuse has an ugly ring to it, Mr Gascoigne.'

A flicker of indecision crossed his features.

Rose raised her head from Antonia's shoulder and smiled wanly. 'Please forget that I mentioned it. I wouldn't want you to get into trouble over me.'

He licked his lips. He was a lost man. He scraped his chair and sprang up. 'Look, I think we can bend the rules just this once.'

Downstairs he hurried them past the trolley-pushers to an unoccupied space between the racks. 'As you probably know, this depot was established early in the war, when Churchill realized the havoc that would be caused if the building in Storey's Gate was bombed. Now I think we have more capacity than they do. We handle just about every item of government stationery. I am the despatch officer.'

'You must be kept busy.'

He smiled disdainfully.

Rose turned to one of the stacks. 'What are these?'

'Leaflets about swine fever. Everything along here relates to agriculture. Not much to interest a lady.'

She asked whether the numbers painted in white on the base of the rack were significant and he started telling her about the classification system.

Rose cut in. 'There must be a list of all these numbers somewhere.'

'There is. I'll show you.'

As they followed him to the end of the rack Rose tapped Antonia's arm. 'See you at the car.'

She stood for a minute or so in front of the plan and index displayed on the end wall —long enough to learn that the Registration of Births, Marriages and Deaths section was in Rows GRO1 to 6 and that Form 134/B (Disposal) was stored in GRO6. Gascoigne was running his finger down the list pointing out items that they might have come across as housewives.

Rose sidled around the end of the nearest rack, turned and walked away, up the column towards the far end. As soon as she reckoned Gascoigne wouldn't see her if he turned round she stepped out fast. She relied on Antonia to invent some excuse.

She slowed to pass two people with trolleys. They didn't give her a second look. She could imagine how easy it would be to get into a zombie-like state pushing a trolley up and down these aisles. Whichever one you chose the scene was the same: dark shelves reaching almost to infinity and lit at intervals by lamps with conical shades coated in dust.

The system also made strong demands on one's concentration. She reckoned the racks marked GRO ought to have been about halfway along, but she'd gone three-quarters of the way and still hadn't found them. She stopped, not wanting to panic, yet fearing she was in error. If she retraced her steps she had no certainty of doing any better. Her shoulders went tense and she breathed faster. Couldn't stand still. Had to look as if she knew what she was doing.

She turned and went back the way she

had come, along the ends of the rows, checking the code numbers. About the middle she became convinced that she was wasting precious time. None of the GRO numbers was there. She would have noticed the first time.

Then she raised her eyes and saw a set of letters and figures much higher up the rack she was standing beside. Because she'd first noticed the information at eye level she hadn't looked any higher. There was a whole series she'd missed. Encouraged, she moved on and found the rack marked GRO6 just a short way ahead. She reached out and ran her hand along one of the shelves. Now all she had to do was find 134/B (Disposal).

The stationery itself was not on view. It was stored in brown paper packets with the coding written on labels pasted on to the ends. She moved along the rack reading them off.

134/B. She clenched her fist in triumph, or relief.

Her idea was to unwrap the top packet, remove a disposal form and tuck it into her handbag. With some care she prised her fingernail under the fold to separate it without causing a tear.

'Are you looking for something?'

A man had come up behind her.

She gasped and spun round.

'What are you doing, exactly?' He wasn't one of the trolley-pushers. He was in a suit like Gascoigne. An important-looking man with silver hair and a black moustache.

A surge of fear galvanized Rose. A lie sprang readily to her lips. 'I was sent over from Somerset House. They ran out of 134/Bs. Mr Gascoigne told me where to find them.'

'Ah. Gascoigne.'

'Here they are. Good.' She tucked a packet under her arm and set off at as brisk a walk as she dared towards the far end of the warehouse and the exit. She wouldn't stop if he called out. There was such a pounding in her head that she wouldn't hear anyway.

She stared ahead, knowing she was trapped if anyone chose to block her path. It was the recurring nightmare of being chased up a narrow passageway, thinking she could make it to the end and then being met by a leaping tiger. Or, in this case, Gascoigne. But he didn't appear. She turned right and headed for the swing doors without a glance to either side. People were moving about there and she avoided looking at them. Through the doors and into the corridor.

Walk.

It was longer than she remembered. God, she thought, I hope I picked the right doors. And then, oh, no, what am I going to tell the doorman?

He turned to face her as she burst through the doors. 'Everything all right?'

'Yes.' She smacked her hand over the label on the packet. 'I got the things.'

'You seem to have lost your friend.'

'Oh, she's following. Got talking to someone. 'Bye, then.'

'Best of luck.'

She'd already had more of that than she was entitled to expect.

28

THROUGH the rear-view mirror of the Bentley, Rose's eyes were fixed on the farthest pillar in a row of housefronts at one end of Lowndes Square, the point where she would first catch sight of somebody approaching from the Stationery Office Depot. She had the engine running and her hands gripping the wheel.

Please God let it be Antonia, she thought. Yet how absurd. She was sitting here waiting for the woman who had tried to chloroform her, who would surely have murdered her, whatever she claimed afterwards. A callous, unpredictable killer for whose arrival Rose was praying fervently. She had no illusions about Antonia. The charm was totally resistible now. Remarks that once seemed witty left her cold, yet she couldn't ignore the certainty that she herself was destined for the gallows if Antonia was arrested and persuaded to confess. What a mess! She didn't see any way to untangle herself.

So she waited in the car.

Two more minutes went by. Rose drummed her fingers on the rim of the wheel.

Then Antonia appeared, her fair hair springing against the black velvet collar as she clattered around the corner in her high heels. She flashed a wide smile when their eyes met. Bravado, Rose thought sourly as she leaned across and lifted the lock on the door, but smiled back.

Antonia hauled it open, sank into the seat and swung her legs in.

'Any joy?'

'Behind you.'

Antonia turned, looked at the packet of

forms on the back seat and whistled. 'Hell's bells, Rosie, we only needed one.'

'It was easier to take the packet.'

'Five hundred! Gordon Bennett! Are you going into business?' She started to laugh.

Rose joined in the peal of giggles, a frankly hysterical reaction as they shattered the tension.

'You don't do things by halves, ducky!'

Their laughter shrilled at least an octave higher, recalling that hilarious moment— Rose had forgotten the cause of the hilarity —in the Black and White Milk Bar just after they had met in Piccadilly. For a few blissful seconds it blotted out everything that had happened since that afternoon.

Someone had to say something when the laughter died and it was Antonia. 'Ah well, who knows, the extra ones may come in useful.'

'What?' Rose almost swung the car into a taxi she was overtaking.

'In case the pen slips and I mess it up, darling.' She gave a chesty laugh. 'What else?'

This time Rose didn't join in.

As they approached the traffic lights at the top of Sloane Street, she returned to practicalities and suggested they stopped somewhere in Hyde Park. 'If we fill the form in right away, we can get to an under-taker's before they close.' She got a nod from Antonia so she turned right, through the Albert Gate into South Carriage Drive. 'How did you cope with Gascoigne?'

'Told him you'd had trouble with your suspenders.'

'Oh, for God's sake.'

'What's up? It was the perfect thing to say. He went pink and twitchy at the thought and his eyes glazed over, dirty old sod, so I knew what to talk about—stocking-tops, belts, garters, corsets and quivering thighs, forests of them. And how to hitch up your stocking with a sixpence. Oh, and the shortage of elastic. That really got his smutty little mind going. The steam was coming out of his ears by then. He forgot all about his precious coding system and he didn't mention you for ten minutes.'

'How did you get away?'

'With ease. When I'd run out of things to say about suspenders I passed on the thought that perhaps we ought to find out whether you were all right. We had a look up and down the aisles, by which time I felt sure you must have found the form and cleared off, so I told Gascoigne that you must have got extremely embarrassed and quit the building minus stockings or worse. He had no difficulty visualizing that. I think he found it very believable. We went down to the entrance and the doorman told us you'd left in a hurry. I winked at Gascoigne and followed you.'

Rose stopped the car. The light was already going and they still had to get to an undertaker's. She fished in her handbag for Barry's fountain pen while Antonia ripped the brown paper off the packet of disposal forms.

'Don't bother, darling. I'd better use mine. I filled in the registration form with it.' She took it out and unscrewed the top. 'Can't be too careful.'

Rose wanted her to concentrate. They couldn't afford a mistake in the form-filling, but Antonia continued to talk. 'There's a dear little undertaker called Hopkinson at the top end of Tottenham Court Road. Much nicer than Greely. We can go straight there and hand him this. Then I'll get you to come home with me and see if Hector's any easier to move before they come for him. It *would* look more natural if he was lying in bed. By now he ought to be more pliable, didn't he?'

'I've no idea.'

'I will need your pen after all. There's

a short bit here that I'm supposed to fill in as myself. Different ink, you see, and bolder handwriting. No flies on me. What was I about to say? Yes, after you've helped me upstairs with Hector I suggest we shake hands and go our different ways.'

'I'm all for that.'

'Fine, but don't sound so bloody pleased about it, my flower. I'm not looking for gratitude for what I did, but you don't have to treat me like a case of measles. Considering the mess your marriage was in when we met, you haven't come out of it at all badly.' She returned the pen to Rose. 'Do you want to check it? The other part has to be filled in by the undertaker.'

'What?' Rose felt a tightening in her stomach. 'What did you say? Let me see.'

'Part C. Part A is the registrar's bit authorizing the disposal, which I've filled in. Part B is for the informant to complete. That's me, and I've done it. And C is for the undertaker. "Notification of Disposal". Oh my God!' She clapped her hand to her mouth.

Rose quietly studied Part C. 'A person disposing of a body must within ninety-six hours deliver to the registrar this notification as to the date, place and means of the disposal of the body.' She was churning inside, but she spoke mechanically, chanting out the obvious as if she were playing consequences, except that it felt and sounded like the death sentence. 'Who does the undertaker notify? The registrar. And the registrar checks it against his records. And if it's a name that doesn't appear in his records, he wants to know why. When he doesn't get a satisfactory answer he asks the police to investigate.' She paused. 'You know, Antonia, we've had it. This perfect murder is a perfect dud.'

'Bloody hell!' Antonia screwed up the paper and drummed her fists against the dashboard. 'Five hundred sodding forms and we can't use one of them.'

Rose didn't have that much energy left. She turned on the engine and drove out of the park, into the traffic moving up Park Lane. She was incapable of saying any more. She was blitzed. It was all she could do, all she wanted to do, to perform the mindless functions of controlling the car. It was some kind of link with normality, like hanging out washing the morning after an air raid that had shattered every window in the house.

Mercifully Antonia also went silent.

The street lights were on already. Outside

the Dorchester a man was selling evening papers. Rose switched on the headlamps as she swung the Bentley into Oxford Street and the predictable jam. While they were inching towards Oxford Circus the subversive aroma of roast chestnuts wafted from a street corner.

'It's past teatime.'

'Shall we?'

'A bag of chestnuts won't go far.'

They stopped at Yarner's in Langham Place and sat by an upstairs window at one of the glass-topped tables with a pot of tea in front of them. They had a corpse at home to dispose of and they blandly ordered Bismarck Herring sandwiches, buttered crumpets and chocolate cake from the silver-haired waitress in her black dress, pink apron and cap. The imminent prospect of returning to the house without the slightest idea what to do with Hector appalled them both. Tea was a convenient hiatus. They didn't speak, except to place the order and pay the bill. They were long past the point of small talk.

Back in the car, Rose handed across a cigarette and lit one herself. 'It's got to be faced. You can't use an undertaker now.'

'What do you mean—*you?*'

'All right. Slip of the tongue. We're in this together.'

Another half-minute passed.

Antonia said, 'Nobody knows he's dead except you and me.'

'And Mr Greely.'

'That undertaker? He didn't use my name once. He'll forget all about us.'

'Some hopes! I should think you're in-delibly fixed in his memory. I can't imagine anyone else has ever changed their mind in a funeral parlour.'

'Greely might remember me, but he didn't meet Hector, did he?'

'You'd better tell me what you're driving at.'

Antonia blew out a thin plume of smoke. Suddenly the bleak look had slipped from her features and was supplanted by an expression Rose had seen before, that afternoon they were standing outside the Ritz—lips pressed together into a secret smile, pleased with itself and scornful of the world, eyes slightly glazed and looking at nothing in par-ticular. 'Hector will just have to disappear.'

Rose frowned.

'Go missing, darling. Plenty do.'

'That's going to take some believing. He wasn't the type.'

'What?'

'Successful businessmen don't go missing. How are you going to account for it?'

'I won't. It's not my job.'

'But you'll have to notify the police.'

'Eventually.'

'And?'

'I'll tell them he didn't come home one night.'

Rose shook her head and sighed. 'It's not much good, Antonia. What are they supposed to think?'

'Anything you bloody well like.' Antonia rattled off a list. 'He fell down a manhole. He lost his memory. He was robbed and pushed into the river. He refused to pay protection money to a gang. He seduced the entire Luton Girls' Choir and fled the country. He got religion and went into—'

Rose cut in. 'For God's sake, Antonia! How will you get rid of the body?'

'*We*, my little helpmate.'

'We, then.'

Antonia waved a dismissive hand. 'Bury him somewhere. Out in the country. A Surrey wood.'

'Have you any idea how hard it is to dig a grave in uncultivated ground?'

'Why? Have you?'

Rose gave her a glare that would have sunk a battleship. 'The newspaper reports always say the victim was found in a shallow grave.'

'What's your suggestion?'

'I don't have one.' Any minute they would be at each other's throats. 'All right. We'll go back to the house.' She succeeded in sounding calm, but her hands shook when she tried fitting the key into the ignition. She didn't know which was worse, the hostility from Antonia or the terror boiling inside herself.

She drove slowly up Portland Place and brought the car round the Devonshire Street turn to the Mews. Antonia got out and ran into the house. Rose pulled out the key of the car and followed.

Antonia's voice hailed her excitedly from the sitting room where they had left the body. 'He's starting to loosen up. I think we can move him tonight.'

Rose thought, what's the point? She remained in the kitchen, sparing herself another sight of the corpse.

Antonia appeared again, radiant with her discovery. Her dead husband might have been a bread-mix from the way she talked about him. 'I'll put some heat in there and he'll be ready in no time.'

Rose looked round for something else to occupy her. The cat had walked in and wanted feeding, so she opened the fridge. Some uncooked meat was in there on a plate. 'Is it safe to feed this to Raffles?'

'What do you mean—safe?'

'Free from poison.'

'For crying out loud, you halfwit. There was never any poison.'

'No poison?'

'Only the chloroform.'

'For Hector?'

'No—for you, stupid.' The barb sprang from Antonia's tongue and she immediately tried to cover it with words. 'The point is, you can feed the bloody cat with perfect safety. I've got to find an electric fire.' She quit the room.

Rose stood rigid. Now she knew. Hector's murder had been an afterthought, one of Antonia's devil-may-care decisions after the murder attempt failed. The whole charade of Antonia going away and Hector requiring cooked meals had been dreamed up to bring Rose herself to the house to be chloroformed and killed.

Why?

How could she have so antagonized Antonia? The worst she was guilty of was an innocent meal out with Hector.

What did Antonia hope to gain by it?

She thought back to Barry's death. That had been casual and coldblooded. Barry had been insufferable, but not to Antonia. She had no grudge against him, yet she had calmly offered to kill him. And kept her promise.

Antonia didn't need a bloodlust or a brainstorm. She murdered with detachment. Yet not without reason. Surely not without reason.

She must have killed Barry because it put Rose under an obligation to her. Something was wanted in return.

The opportunity to steal the death certificate from the registrar? Not just that.

Rose clenched her fists.

My identity.

I assumed all along that she wanted me to square the account by killing Hector, possibly without knowing what I was doing. I was wrong. If she'd wanted Hector dead she'd have done it herself. She didn't need me for that. But if she killed me she could write her own name on the death certificate and 'die'. She'd have my handbag with all my papers and my house keys. She'd become Rose Bell and she'd be free to go to America with Vic and marry him.

And Hector, could he have known about this? Was it possible that he'd gone along with it? Did he know of the plan that evening in Reggiori's?

Rose thought back to what she had heard about the drowning of Hector's first wife. He'd connived at that. Why shouldn't he have also connived at another murder?

The cat mewed.

She took the meat from the fridge and looked for a knife with a good, sharp edge.

29

'JUST what are you doing with that knife?'

Antonia stood in the doorway, her right hand gripping the door frame.

Rose looked up. She'd taken it from a drawer containing wooden spoons, tin openers, meat skewers and a selection of knives and cleavers. This had been the obvious one to choose, a long bone-handled carver with a blade that may once have been uniformly wide. Years of sharpening had honed it to a point.

'What I said I would do—cutting up meat for the cat.'

'It shouldn't be used for that.'

'Why not? It's wonderfully sharp.'

'It's the carver.'

'I've finished now.' Calmly Rose picked up the chopping board and used the knife to push the pieces off into the cat's dish. 'That should keep him quiet.' She took the knife to the sink and ran some water over it. She reached for a teacloth and wiped the blade, taking care not to touch the edge, turning it over appreciatively. 'An old knife like this is certainly worth looking after.'

'Why do you say that?'

Rose gave a shrug. 'I wouldn't mind betting it's sharper than anything else you've got.'

For a moment Antonia had looked alarmed. Now she seemed to accept that she'd misinterpreted what she'd seen. She put her hand to her hair and twined one blonde strand around her forefinger and twitched her mouth into an odd, speculative smile. 'There's a hacksaw in the garage.'

Rose frowned. 'What's that got to do with it?'

'I should have thought it was obvious.'

'Well, it isn't to me. What are you suggesting?'

'He'd be easier to bury in pieces.'

Rose dropped the knife in the drawer and slammed it shut.

Antonia carried on in a persuasive voice as if she were suggesting how to pass a diverting evening. 'We could wrap the bits in newspaper and bury them in different places.'

'That's vile. How could you possibly do it?'

'The two of us, ducky.'

Rose's stomach heaved. 'You must be mad even to think of such a horrible thing.'

She got a cold stare. 'Think of something better, then.' Getting no answer, Antonia added, 'Sweetie, we've got a dead man to dispose of. You'd better face up to reality.'

The words hit Rose hard. The thought of butchering any human corpse, let alone Hector's, was too nauseous to contemplate. Yet she was barren of suggestions.

As if to underline the inactivity, Antonia fetched some playing cards from one of the other rooms and started a game of patience on the kitchen table.

'Understand what I said, Rose? You kept your lily white hands clean when I got rid

of Barry, but you're as tainted as I am because you asked me to do it. I don't know
what goes on inside that mind of yours, but
you can't go on looking the other way. Face
it, you're a killer, just as I am. If you want
to go on living, stop playing Snow White
and get some blood on your hands.'

The phone rang.

Their eyes met. Antonia stood up. 'It'll be
Vic.'

'Don't answer it.'

'I can talk to Vic.'

'You don't know who it is.'

The bell pealed out its insistent notes.

'For pity's sake, it's only a telephone.'
Antonia ran across the hall.

'You're asking for trouble.'

Furious, Rose followed her into the room
and stood not a yard away.

'Yes? . . . Speaking, yes.' Antonia switched
the receiver to her other ear and turned her
back on Rose. Her voice was guarded. This
certainly wasn't Vic. 'Really? He left here
as usual . . . . No, not yet, but that's nothing unusual. He works all hours, as you
know . . . . I see . . . . No, he didn't—but
then I didn't enquire. I'm his wife, darling,
not his nursemaid. Perhaps he spent the day
at that exhibition . . . . Closed? I didn't

know that . . . . Well, did he go to Paris, do you think? He had lunch with some Frenchman the other day . . . . God, no, I'd be the last to know . . . . Listen, my dear, it's not the end of the world. Surely the place can survive for a couple of days without him? I'll get him to ring you if he gets in touch. There's nothing more I can do.' She slammed down the phone. 'Bloody woman.'

'His secretary?'

'Fussing over sweet F.A., as usual. What time is it?'

'Just gone nine.'

'A fine time to call me. I've got my suspicions about Hector and that girl.'

'She's got suspicions of her own by the sound of it.'

'Piffle. She doesn't know there's anything wrong.'

'That's beside the point, Antonia. He's been missed at work already. If you're going to play the anxious wife you'll have to call the police damn quick.'

Antonia slid her eyes in the direction of the drawing room where the corpse was lying. 'How can I?'

Rose had no answer. She'd rejected everything Antonia had suggested.

In her mind's eye she stood over Hector's body with a hacksaw, bracing herself to use it. Revolting. Yet it was rapidly coming to that.

No. She'd reached her sticking-point. 'There must be another way of dealing with this. A better way.'

'Well?' Antonia waited with the air of a schoolmistress expecting some glib answer.

Out of sheer desperation Rose talked, casting for ideas as she spoke. 'We take everything out of his pockets that could be used to identify him.'

'We'd have to do that whatever happened.'

'Let me finish. And then we put him in the boot of the car and drive out and . . . find a bomb site that hasn't been cleared.'

'A bomb site—that's a thought.'

Confidence surged through Rose like a drug. 'We drop him into a hole and cover it with rubble. The chances are that he'll never be found. If he is, they'll think he was looting and had an accident. Or that he was just some tramp using it as a place to sleep.'

Antonia made a fist and feigned a punch. 'Brilliant, Rosie! Let's drink to it.' She fetched two glasses and a bottle of the Burgundy, which she uncorked with one pull of the corkscrew. 'Just one. Got to stay on our feet.'

They touched glasses. Antonia's eyes may have caught some reflected light from the cut glass but it seemed to Rose that they shone with something more than relief. There was a gleam of triumph there. Almost of rapture. It was as if she was looking ahead to some sort of happy-ever-after.

Rose brusquely recalled her to the present. 'Croydon is the place. I come through there when I visit my parents. It's peppered with bomb sites.'

'Croydon?' Antonia spoke the name as if it were Timbuktu. 'We don't need to go that far when you've got a perfectly good site in Pimlico, darling.'

'Where?'

'Christ Almighty, if *you* don't know . . . .'

Rose gazed at her in disbelief. 'You can't mean Oldfield Gardens.'

'You bet I do. It hasn't been cleared, has it?'

'I am not going to bury Hector in Oldfield Gardens.'

Antonia rebuked Rose in a good-natured way. 'Don't be such a sap. It's the ideal place. It's not overlooked.'

'No. I refuse. It's much too near. It would be asking for trouble.'

'That great poster screens it from the road.'

'We're taking him to Croydon.'

Antonia conceded tamely. 'Have it your way if you insist, darling.'

Rose went out to the car. She had remembered the packet of disposal forms on the back seat. She brought them back to the house, gave them to Antonia and told her to make a fire of them. Antonia took them off to the drawing room, joking that if they helped to raise the temperature a few degrees the afternoon hadn't been a complete waste of time. She was in a better mood now that they'd settled what to do with Hector, and she seemed appreciative of Rose's more positive role.

Some time towards midnight Antonia came back to the kitchen. She'd changed into a sweater and slacks and she'd brought some down for Rose and dumped them on the table, together with a pair of flat shoes.

'You can't climb over bomb sites in heels.'

It was sensible. The things were dark blue in colour, too. Rose changed while Antonia went off to take another look at the body. She could have done with a size smaller in slacks, but the shoes fitted well. She was thankful to get out of her own things for the task ahead. It was like being back in uniform, which had always given her the

feeling she was part of something impersonal, at several removes from her real life.

30

ANTONIA called out breezily that the body
was ready to move.

Rose felt the gooseflesh rise again. Resolved to master her nerves, she reached for
the wine bottle, poured herself some more
and swallowed it at a gulp. 'Coming.'

She joined Antonia in the drawing room.
This time she didn't flinch at the sight of
the body. She did what Antonia had urged,
faced up to reality and forced herself to
take in the scene as if it were a waxwork
tableau. More colour remained in Hector's
features than she would have expected. Perhaps the chloroform had roughened his
cheeks. Antonia had already removed some
money from the pockets and placed it on a
table nearby, together with a wallet, a handkerchief and a set of keys. No one could
possibly identify Hector now, she claimed
confidently.

'Ready, then?' Rose said. They were act-
ing on her initiative now. She was taking
charge.

Antonia nodded. It was almost as if she welcomed the secondary role.

They bent over the body and took a grip. The muscles were noticeably less rigid now. There was some movement at the knees and hips.

Antonia took most of the weight, slotting her hands under the armpits. They stumbled to the door and across the hall, pausing outside the kitchen. In two more stages they lifted him out to the garage. The torso was difficult to get into the car boot, so Rose lifted the legs in first and then supported the small of the back as they heaved him inside.

She shut down the lid and leaned on it.

'How's the time?'

'It must be after midnight. Rose, how long will it take to get there?'

'Getting on for three-quarters of an hour. And then we've got to scout around for a place to leave him.'

'Let's fetch our coats, then.'

At the door on the way out, Antonia gave a girlish shriek of laughter. 'What on earth are you bringing your handbag for?'

'It's got everything in it. My ration book. My identity card.'

'Rosie, you'll be the death of me. We're not going shopping and we don't want to be identified. Leave it behind. All we need is the key of the car.'

'I forgot.' Rose turned and threw the bag on to the kitchen table, annoyed at her own stupidity. To reassert herself she announced that she would do the driving. Antonia didn't object.

Great Portland Street was almost deserted. Only when they approached the Oxford Circus end did they start seeing people in evening clothes standing far out in the road to try and hail one of the few taxis operating at that hour. Some waved at anything on four wheels and shouted their fury at being ignored. A fine drizzle was adding to their discomfort.

Rose switched on the wipers and glanced at the petrol gauge. They had ample. The Bentley fairly purred compared with the RAF staff cars she was used to handling. She took the route through Piccadilly Circus and the Haymarket towards Charing Cross, then followed the river as far as Vauxhall Bridge. At the lights she said she wouldn't mind a cigarette.

Antonia didn't respond.

'I said have you got a fag?'

'What, darling?'

'A cigarette. My handbag is back at the house. Remember?'

Antonia found a packet of her wicked-smelling Abdullahs in the glove compartment.

'Thanks. You were miles away.'

'Mm.'

'Thinking about America?'

'What?'

'America. Princeton, isn't it?'

Antonia tensed beside her. The voice shed its mateyness. 'How do you know about that?'

The lights changed. Rose eased from second into third and they started to cross the bridge. 'Hector told me. Wasn't I supposed to know?'

Antonia started justifying herself rapidly. 'It doesn't matter a damn. I can't go now. I can't get married again, not while Hec is officially missing. It takes years and years before the law will admit that a missing person is dead. I can't marry again, and Vic won't even talk about living together. I thought this country was the last word in prudishness, but it seems they're just as narrow-minded in New Jersey.'

Rose drove on without comment.

Antonia only pressed her case more

vigorously. 'Didn't I tell you about this? Believe me, there wasn't any question of trying to keep it from you. I mean, why should I, darling? I introduced you to Vic. God, after what you and I have been through together, we don't need to hide anything from each other.'

Rose had stopped listening. Something bloody underhanded was going on. She'd touched a raw nerve when she mentioned America. Antonia's pacifying gush was more of a threat than outright hostility. All this reassurance couldn't paper over the fact that Vic and his job in Princeton were still paramount in Antonia's plans. It was screamingly obvious that she hadn't given up the idea. She was resolved to go to America with him. How could she, without marrying him?

Stockwell came up, then Brixton. They swung into the Brixton Road. Not much was moving in either direction. It was tempting to take the Bentley up to higher speeds along the wide highway, but she dared not risk it. This was the time of night when police cars lay in wait in side roads.

Heavier rain than they had been through had saturated the road. Each streetlamp stood over its own reflection and each oncoming car appeared to have four headlamps. The wet tyres rustled and clicked. Don't let it lull you into quiescence, Rose told herself. This is the most dangerous hour of your life.

The first sign for Croydon came up.

Antonia rubbed at the window with her hand. 'Journey's end, my flower.'

Rose drove on. Most of the bombing had been further in, and she had a particular site in mind. A street close to West Croydon Station had been devastated by one of the giant V2 rockets in 1944. The entire area had since been evacuated and fenced round with corrugated iron, but children had ripped down a section of the fence to make their own cycle speedway track where there had been private gardens. Shells of houses stood about waiting for demolition, long since looted of anything worth owning. Clumps of willowherb and yellow ragwort had sprouted where pavements had been.

The turn came up on the left. For a short stretch they drove on the regular road past houses where people slept. The street lighting was sparse. Then the Bentley's headlamps picked out the gap she had re-membered in the fence at the far end. There was space enough for the car to pass through, out of sight of the houses. It swayed and rocked across a pitted surface on to the remains of a road until they were forced to stop where a wall had collapsed.

Antonia flung open the door and got out. 'Wonderful, darling!' She stood in the rain with her arms folded, relishing the scene as if it were Epsom Downs on Derby Day. 'Let's go prospecting, shall we? There's a torch on the back seat.'

Rose couldn't understand this boisterousness. Nerves affected people in unexpected ways, but was this a case of nerves? Was the Benzedrine responsible? She switched off the headlamps and shone the torch across the site. Two years' growth of weeds had covered the rubble and made the footing awkward. Antonia was already striding indomitably towards the nearest ruined houses, which were—or had been—semi-detached, the sort that aspiring middle class people owned. Probably they had once been allotted numbers that the owners had replaced with names like *Mon Repos*. They stood roofless and derelict. Rose shone the torch upwards. Where bits of wall jutted out of the debris were traces of floral wallpaper.

The first two houses were impenetrable. Presumably to keep children out, boards had been hammered across the doorways and window spaces and crisscrossed with taut barbed wire. They picked their way around them with the torch until even Antonia's optimism faltered.

'We're wasting our time if they're all like this.'

Rose refused to be beaten. This was her show now. She was no longer passive. She had forced her personality out of its strait-jacket and she had a liking for liberty. She pointed the torch behind them, across what had once been the garden. 'What's that, then?'

The small circle of light had stopped on a dark, raised mass.

'Just rubbish.'

Certainly when Rose stepped closer she found a collection of rusting and broken objects that must have been heaped there during the salvage operation. A garden roller without its wooden handle, several dented saucepans, a piece of saturated, threadbare carpet, a wheelbarrow, the frame of a deck-chair. She stooped to examine something that gleamed. It was a chromium-plated key-plate.

Antonia came over. 'What have you found?'

'Somebody's front door by the look of it. Help me slide it to one side.'

'What for? Is there something underneath?'

'I don't know. There might be.' Rose had noticed a patch of concrete and a curved piece of corrugated steel that suggested a possibility.

Together they gripped the edge of the door and tried to move it.

'There's too much heavy stuff on top.'

They scrabbled among the rubbish and lifted off a few bricks and a coalbucket filled with china fragments. At the second attempt they succeeded in pulling the door about a yard to one side.

Antonia whistled. 'Nice work, darling!'

They had uncovered three or four steps leading underground to a cavity blocked by more rubbish, the frame of a pushchair and a dustbin lid.

'Who would have known it?' said Antonia.

They had found an Anderson shelter, the fortified hole in the ground that millions of families had installed in their gardens in the first years of the war, consisting of a curved arch of corrugated steel sunk three feet and covered with earth. This one had partially collapsed and was so overgrown as to be barely recognizable.

Together they hauled out the objects that were blocking the entrance. Then they used the torch again. The steel walls had become unclamped at the top and now sagged. The space inside was much reduced.

'It doesn't look very safe.'

'Doesn't need to be,' said Rose.

She picked up a stone and tossed it in. They heard it bounce across the concrete floor. Antonia grabbed the torch and crouched to peer inside. Her voice had a promising echo. 'Darling, it's ideal. His own tomb. We can cover him with rubble and put back the rubbish and no one will ever find him. When they clear the site they'll just bulldoze this. Let's fetch him, shall we? Have you got the keys?'

Rose handed them over as if to a servant. She felt elated at having solved the problem of where to deposit the body. She was entitled to some self-congratulation. She alone had thought of this place and found the shelter. Without her, Antonia wouldn't have stood a chance of getting away with murder. As it was, Hector's body was most unlikely to be found. He would just be listed as a missing person, one of thousands. And the credit for that belonged to her.

Mustn't get over complacent, she thought immediately. The night isn't over yet. She followed Antonia to the car.

Antonia had already turned the key and

lifted the boot lid. They reached into the dark interior and hauled out the body and staggered towards the garden containing the shelter. The distance they had to cover was about seventy yards, and the footing was treacherous. Either of them could easily have turned an ankle. As it was, they managed it without a rest, pausing only when they stood by the steps of the shelter. They set the body down with the head and shoulders resting on the door.

'Get some breath back first.' Rose took a seat on the steps.

'As you wish.' Antonia took the torch from her pocket and started shining it over the rubbish around them.

'Looking for something?'

'Nothing in particular.'

Rose didn't believe her. She was capable of anything.

Antonia said, 'Feet first, I reckon.'

'What?'

'When we lift him in, his feet should go first.'

Rose didn't comment. Her eyes were following the beam of the torch. It picked out a set of rusty fire irons lying loose beside the wheelbarrow. Tongs, a shovel and a poker. The beam danced on to something else, coaxing her attention that way. Some instinct made her resist. Instead she turned her gaze back, outside the pool of light, and saw Antonia put her foot against the poker and covertly nudge it closer to the shelter entrance.

'Are you listening, Rose?'

Suddenly the torch was shining full in her face. She stiffened like a rabbit caught in a headlight's glare, except that the paralysing terror struck her a moment before the light. She managed to whisper, 'What?'

'Ready to start?'

Rose put up her arm protectively. 'Stop it. It's dazzling me.

'Get up, then.'

The beam moved away and the immediate feeling of helplessness passed. Rose had her hand to her eyes and she looked between the fingers to where the poker was lying. She'd expected Antonia to make a grab for it. Not yet, apparently. But she would at the next opportunity. 'If you want his legs to go into the shelter first, you can lift them. I'm not going right inside.'

'Why not?' demanded Antonia. 'You're smaller than I am.

'I don't like small spaces.'

Antonia lowered the torch and held it

out to her. 'Look inside. It's all right. No rats or anything. Get a grip on yourself, you great sissy.'

'That's enough!' Rose sprang up and pushed a warning finger at Antonia's face. 'I could easily walk away and leave you now.'

The tone switched abruptly from scorn to protest. 'But you've refused all along to lift him by the shoulders.'

'Never mind. I'm ready to do it now.'

'Oh, for Christ's sake! Have it your way, ducky, but let's get on with it.'

Antonia dropped the torch and strutted histrionically past Rose to take a grip on Hector's legs. But the bluster didn't succeed as a diversion. Rose kept her eyes on the poker. She watched Antonia locate it with her right foot and glance down and attempt to nudge it out of sight under some thistles. Proof positive that she would launch an attack with it any minute. One or two blows on the skull with that would be death.

Disposing of Hector wasn't enough. Antonia meant to kill again.

Why?

Rose knew why.

It's the same plan as before, only this time she's streamlined it. She means to kill me and take over my identity. She'll bury me here, with Hector's corpse. She's got my handbag at home with my keys, my ration book and my identity card. She can get into my house and find my birth certificate and anything else she needs. She'll use my name to get married to Vic. And then she'll go to America with him.

She will not.

Rose forced herself to stand up, step woodenly across the rubble and take up the position she had said she would, facing Antonia, with the length of Hector's body between them. This was the task that had to be completed, whatever else happened. Neither could manage it alone.

She stooped and slid her hands under the back, between the arms. Then she looked at Antonia, who was dipping to take the weight of the legs. They nodded at each other like two removal men lifting a piece of furniture.

Rose knew that the minute her usefulness was at an end, when Hector's corpse was safely in the shelter, Antonia would attack. She definitely meant to kill.

And if by some chance the bodies of a man and a woman were discovered here later, the woman with an impacted skull, she would be dressed in clothes that had belonged to

Antonia. The cunning that had ordered the events of the past few hours was clear.

Rose shuffled forward bearing the main weight of the body, eyes downcast as if she couldn't bear the sight of poor Hector's face. Actually her reason for looking down had more to do with self-interest: she was coming to the place where the poker was lying. She made a performance of stumbling slightly when she reached the thistles. It enabled her to nudge her right foot under the poker and push it at least a couple of feet aside.

Antonia seemed not to have noticed. She was making her way backwards down the three concrete steps, dipping low under the steel roof. She was right inside the shelter as Rose came down the steps. Funny. She obviously felt safe. She'd never considered Rose as a physical threat.

'All right?'

'Yes.'

They lowered their burden to the concrete floor.

Neither added a word. The silence wasn't out of respect for the dead.

Now.

Rose turned and stretched across the concrete to reach for the poker. Her fingertips made contact with the handle. She took a grip, turned back towards the shelter entrance and raised her arm high behind her shoulder.

Antonia was bowing low to come out. There wasn't much light to see her by, but the pale arch of her hair was discernible, and as she lifted her face the eyes appeared colourless. There was an instant when those eyes sighted Rose, a split second of disbelief.

Rose swung the poker and crashed it into the blonde head with more force than she knew she possessed.

Antonia slumped forward, across Hector's body. Probably that first blow killed her, but there was too much bitterness, too much resentment to be contained in one blow. Rose battered Antonia repeatedly about the head. She sobbed as she struck and the sobs kept the rhythm of the blows for some time before she exhausted herself, slowed and stopped.

31

A long silence.

Rose was incapable of telling how long she remained on her knees with her hands over her eyes. Eventually she sensed that the shaking of her body wasn't so much from a sense of shock as from cold. Her coat was saturated. Fine rain still lashed down. She stood up stiffly and looked down at what she had done.

And felt more relieved than regretful.

I am safe from her. Whatever I am guilty of, I am safe from her. She can't hurt me now.

And nor can anyone else if I cover the bodies, bury them under the rubble. Somehow I must raise the strength.

She picked up the torch and trudged up the steps and looked about her. The circle of light travelled over the ground, searching. It stopped at a black area that the weeds had failed to colonize. She went closer and found a folded piece of tarpaulin attached to a length of timber, all that was left of somebody's coalshed. As she bent to take a grip, a large frog hopped out from under the fold, but she didn't recoil. She lifted a corner and disturbed other things that would normally have repelled her, woodlice, beetles and centipedes. She was unmoved. She had a new scale of horrors now. With the aid of a rusty old tyre lever that came to hand, she prised and tore the tarpaulin away from the wood. Then she dragged it across the site to the shelter and down the steps.

Before covering the bodies she knelt and used her sleeve to wipe some smudges from Hector's forehead. His eyes were closed and the pale lashes were damp from the rain. He still had the look of an overgrown cherub. She thought for a moment of that remark Antonia had made about mothering him. But you really fancied me, didn't you, Hec, she thought. Then she drew the tarpaulin gently over his face and tucked it under his shoulder, separating him from the face-down corpse of Antonia with its skullcap of blood.

She got up and set about collecting rubble to bury them with, heaping whatever she could lift into the void and hearing it slap against the tarpaulin. The bulky things that she and Antonia had pulled out, the coal bucket, the pushchair and the dustbin lid, helped fill the space. Some chunks of masonry were too heavy, so she rolled them to the steps and toppled them in. Her hands felt sore and her fingernails were in shreds. Her back ached. Still she toiled, going increasingly far from the shelter in search of debris she could handle.

It began to look less like a shelter entrance as she filled it in. She buried the bottom step and then the next. The broken wheelbarrow went in, and part of a wooden fence. More broken bricks and chunks of plaster followed.

As the level of debris in the shelter rose, so did her spirits. Bone-weary she may have been, but she had outsmarted and destroyed the most dangerous woman she was ever likely to meet.

Antonia is lying under three feet of rubble. This is what would have happened to me, she told herself. Instead, I was brave enough to defy her. I met the challenge. I didn't flinch when it was necessary to kill. She tried to destroy me and got destroyed herself. She tried to steal my life, my name, and make it hers. I didn't let her.

I deserve to get away with this.

She picked up the torch and switched it on again to survey the result of her efforts. After an hour or more of heavy work the surface was level. The shelter entrance was practically indistinguishable from the rest of the site. She found the old door that had been lying over the steps and pushed it back into position.

Dead and gone.

She took a long, sustaining breath and stepped wearily across the garden towards the Bentley. She would drive back to Park

Crescent and park the car in its garage in the mews and collect her things. It would be bliss to put on her own clothes again. She'd pick up her handbag and make a parcel of the muddy clothes and drop them somewhere on the way home. She'd be home in Pimlico before dawn.

The car gleamed damply in the torchlight. I wouldn't mind a sleep on the back seat for twenty minutes, she thought. No, that's the sort of stupid thing the old Rose Bell would have done. Can't do that. Antonia wouldn't do that. She'd conquer the fatigue and drive straight back to London, and that's what I shall do. You can only expect to get away with murder if you keep your nerve and master your weaknesses. I was downtrodden and pathetic until a few weeks ago. Not now.

I got rid of Barry and saved myself from Antonia. I came out the winner. The survivor. The merry widow.

I'm stronger, more confident and better off than I have been in the whole of my life. Widow be damned. I'll get a good man, a real catch. See if I don't. What was it Antonia said? With legs like mine I should have heels three inches high.

She had her hand on the car door when a man called out to her.

'Just a minute, miss.'

She turned and looked across the site to the gap in the fence. He was standing there under a streetlamp holding the handlebars of his cycle—a policeman in uniform.

Her heart-rate doubled, but she refused to panic. He doesn't know a thing, she told herself.

His words confirmed it when he wheeled the bike across to her. 'You're out late, miss, or is it early?'

He was under twenty-five, clean-shaven, blue-eyed. Quite a dish, in fact. And the way he was looking at her he might have just asked for a dance.

She laughed.

He took the lamp off the front of his bike and took stock of the Bentley. 'Handsome car. Yours, is it?'

She leaned on the open door with a possessive air. 'Right down to the last rivet, darling. And now you want to know what I'm doing here on a bomb site looking like this. Am I right?'

He grinned.

She had his measure. He was putty. Soon deal with him.

316

'I let my wretched doggie off the lead and he ran in here and that was the last I saw of him. I've been scrambling in and out of dangerous places calling his name for hours. I hope he's all right.'

'He'll probably find his own way home. They usually do. Do you live nearby, miss?'

'No, in London. That's why I'm so worried.' The lies rolled easily off her tongue.

'It's a long way to bring a dog for a walk.'

'Oh, we only stopped for a wee.' She gave him a smile. 'You know what I mean. I've been to Brighton for the evening and I'm on the way home.'

'You've got your clothes in a state, miss.'

'I know, darling. Isn't it a bore? I can't wait to get out of them and into a nice, hot bath. Imagine it!'

He tilted his head to one side. She watched his eyes. He was young. He gave a half-smile—the sap.

'What's the dog's name?'

Quick—a name for a dog. 'Lucky.' She was away now. 'A cross between a bull terrier and a Bedlington, if you can imagine that. Pink eyes and white woolly hair. If ever a dog was misnamed, it's this one.'

'Well, if I hear anything . . . .'

317

'You'll make a certain lady very grateful indeed.'

'What's your name, miss?'

A name for a woman this time. 'Um— Princeton. Vicky Princeton. What's yours?'

He slid his finger under the strap of his helmet.

She said, 'Well, you're flesh and blood, sweetie. You must have a name.'

'We use numbers in the police, Miss Princeton.'

She peered at his collar. '109 is it? I'd rather call you Bobby.'

He said ponderously, 'I'd better make a note of your address, in case someone brings in the dog.'

She laughed and said as if she was being propositioned, 'Oh, yes?'

This wasn't all fun and games. He'd taken out his notebook and pencil.

'Well, I'm staying with friends at the moment. It's a pub. The Prince Regent in Lambeth.'

'That's not your own address, then?'

'It's not my own dog.' She was pleased with that witty riposte. 'It belongs to the landlord. If I'm still there, I'll buy you a drink, Bobby.'

'PC 109, if you don't mind.'

She smiled. 'I don't, if you don't.' And if I'd met you anywhere else, you pushover, it wouldn't have to end with me driving off alone into the night, she thought.

He kept rigidly to his official manner. 'I must ask you to move the vehicle, miss. Strictly speaking, you shouldn't have driven it in here.'

'I was on the point of leaving anyway . . . officer.'

She swung back the door and got in. Closed it. Smiled.

Felt in her coat pocket for the keys.

Her pocket was empty. So was the other one. But she had driven the car here.

He tapped on the window. 'Something the matter, miss?'

'My key?—I can't find them.'

As she said it, she remembered Antonia asking for the keys to open the boot when the two of them had gone to fetch Hector's body. Once the lid was up, Antonia must have pocketed them.

The bloody keys were buried with Antonia.

PC 109 opened the door. 'Let me have a look. They've fallen on the floor, I expect. Step out a minute, would you?'

Rose got out. This was dreadful. Maddening. She considered making a run for it while he got on his knees to search. No, she had to brazen this out.

The beam of his lamp probed the interior. 'Could they be in the back, do you think?'

'It's possible, I suppose.'

As she opened the rear door a ball of paper fell out of the car. She knew what it was at once—the disposal form Antonia had filled in with Hector's name and screwed up in disgust when she saw the part that had to be returned to the registrar.

Bloody Antonia!

She stooped to snatch it up.

Too quickly. Too nervously. Antonia would never have moved so fast.

Reacting to her sudden movement, the policeman reached out and grabbed it first.

'What have we got here, then?'

'Give it to me.' Suddenly the old fears flapped and swooped like vultures. This was dreadful, ruinous. She wasn't going to get away with murder. She was only Rose Bell, the luckless Rose.

'I said what have we got here?'

He flashed the lamp at her, dazzling her. The white light had a strange, disorientating effect. It bleached out the bomb site, the Bentley, the policeman, in fact everything that had happened since she had last been blinded by torchlight. She had a horrid conviction that Antonia was still there, pointing the torch, mocking her.

She screamed. A full-throated, terrified scream.

The policeman lowered the lamp and said quite calmly, 'I think I'd better see what all the fuss is about, don't you, miss?'

He started to unfold the ball of paper.